Corrine Martin Was Dangerous.

Rand emerged from the washroom to find her waiting. He didn't know *why* she made him react the way she did, only that she did. And he didn't like it. He wanted to blast through her icy exterior and make her the vulnerable one, not him—never again.

If she were a different kind of woman, he would take her. But there was no way he'd be able to remain uninvolved with her. Already the tension was intensifying, making him shake with a weakness he refused to acknowledge.

"Hi," she said softly.

Her voice brushed over him, making him feel heavy and lethargic. His groin tightened, and he could only nod at her. He was used to playing and winning, even with women. Winning made him feel in control and sure of himself. But there was a vulnerability in Corrine's eyes that warned this wasn't a game. Or at least not one that would leave behind a victor....

Dear Reader,

Spring into the new season with six fresh passionate, powerful and provocative love stories from Silhouette Desire.

Experience first love with a young nurse and the arrogant surgeon who stole her innocence, in *USA TODAY* bestselling author Elizabeth Bevarly's *Taming the Beastly MD* (#1501), the latest title in the riveting DYNASTIES: THE BARONES continuity series. Another *USA TODAY* bestselling author, Cait London, offers a second title in her HEARTBREAKERS miniseries—*Instinctive Male* (#1502) is the story of a vulnerable heiress who finds love in the arms of an autocratic tycoon.

And don't miss RITA® Award winner Marie Ferrarella's *A Bachelor and a Baby* (#1503), the second book of Silhouette's crossline series THE MOM SQUAD, featuring single mothers who find true love. In *Tycoon for Auction* (#1504) by Katherine Garbera, a lady executive wins the services of a commitment-shy bachelor. A playboy falls in love with his secretary in *Billionaire Boss* (#1505) by Meagan McKinney, the latest MATCHED IN MONTANA title. And a Native American hero's fling with a summer-school teacher produces unexpected complications in *Warrior in Her Bed* (#1506) by Cathleen Galitz.

This April, shower yourself with all six of these moving and sensual new love stories from Silhouette Desire.

Enjoy!

Joan Marlow Golan

Joan Marlow Golan
Senior Editor, Silhouette Desire

Please address questions and book requests to:
Silhouette Reader Service
U.S.: 3010 Walden Ave., P.O. Box 1325, Buffalo, NY 14269
Canadian: P.O. Box 609, Fort Erie, Ont. L2A 5X3

Tycoon for Auction
KATHERINE GARBERA

Published by Silhouette Books
America's Publisher of Contemporary Romance

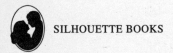 SILHOUETTE BOOKS

ISBN 0-373-76504-5

TYCOON FOR AUCTION

Copyright © 2003 by Katherine Garbera

This edition published by arrangement with Harlequin Books S.A.

Visit Silhouette at www.eHarlequin.com

Printed in U.S.A.

Books by Katherine Garbera

Silhouette Desire

The Bachelor Next Door #1104
Miranda's Outlaw #1169
Her Baby's Father #1289
Overnight Cinderella #1348
Baby at His Door #1367
Some Kind of Incredible #1395
The Tycoon's Temptation #1414
The Tycoon's Lady #1464
Cinderella's Convenient Husband #1466
Tycoon for Auction #1504

KATHERINE GARBERA

lives near Chicago with the man she met in Fantasyland and their two kids. She started writing to prove to herself that she could do it and found herself addicted to it. Creating worlds where everyday people find love and balance it with already full lives appeals to her. She loves revisiting the places that have influenced her and has once again returned to Orlando, which is an especially fond place for the native Floridian. Readers can visit her home page on the Web at www.katherinegarbera.com.

This book is dedicated to Mavis Allen,
for her insight and her laughter.
It's a real pleasure to be working with you!

Acknowledgments

This book is a different direction for me, and I have to
thank many people for the opportunity to try it.
Joan Marlow Golan and Mavis Allen, who pointed out
my first version of the hero was a little weak and then
encouraged me to try something new.

Teresa Brown, Pam Labud and Catherine Kean,
who helped with every Orlando question I had.
Any mistakes are my own. Eve Gaddy, who spent
endless hours on the phone with me talking about this
story and how to make it stronger, plus just offering her
support—the words *thank you* really aren't enough!
And thanks to Nancy Thompson, who double-checked
some facts on Orlando for me.
I wish we could still meet for lunch at Dexters!

As always, thanks to my family for their love and
support, without which I'd probably accomplish nothing.

One

Lust wasn't something Corrine Martin was comfortable admitting she experienced. It didn't fit with the image she'd carefully cultivated—cool sophistication from the top of her blond head to the toes exposed by her slinky gold sandals. She'd done a good job of ignoring the surging feelings and the man who inspired them—until tonight.

Maybe it was something in his wizard-green eyes. Or maybe it was just that she was tired of having him stare through her as if she wasn't there. Whatever the reason, tonight she'd thrown caution to the wind and had purchased Rand Pearson for three corporate dates.

Of course, she'd only bid on his services as a corporate spouse. She even had an airtight excuse for doing it. She needed an escort to the upcoming business meetings she'd be expected to attend.

The ballroom at the Walt Disney Dolphin Hotel had been transformed into an old-fashioned buy-a-bride auction. All the money raised tonight would go to the Collation for the Homeless, an Orlando-based charity that fed and sheltered the homeless. This was Corrine's first year attending. She'd bid on and won the services of Rand Pearson.

Though they'd been working together for the last five months on a training project, she really didn't know him. He'd been one of only three men on the auctioning block representing the company he was a partner in—Corporate Spouses. The company provided business-etiquette lessons as well as dates for executives for business functions.

Corrine's boss, Paul Sterling, the CEO of Tarron Enterprises, had won a similar package the year before. Corrine had been Paul's secretary until his promotion to CEO when Paul had promoted her to a midlevel manager. Corrine loved the challenge her new role provided.

But she needed to show her boss that she wasn't in danger of becoming one-dimensional and focused only on her job as a middle manager at Tarron Enterprises. And on a more personal level she needed to remind herself that she was still a woman.

Rand Pearson made her feel dangerous and alive. She didn't like it, but she knew she needed to deal with it and get her life back on track. She had her eye on the vacant vice president position and knew that she'd need to be focused one hundred percent at work.

"Dance with me, Corrine?" Rand asked, coming up to her. His tuxedo was obviously custom-made, making him look like royalty, which, if gossip was true, he'd descended from.

"Why?" she asked. She'd never had any finesse when it came to men. They made her nervous. Probably because of her experiences in foster care during her teen years.

"When a man asks you to dance, Cori, yes or no is the appropriate answer," he said, with that gleam in his eyes that made her want to do something shocking. Which was how she'd ended up bidding on him.

She sighed and reminded herself that she was known as the ice queen for a very good reason. Life was safer that way. "My name is Corrine. And I know that."

"Do you?" He slid closer to her in the crowded ballroom. His hand glided up her arm—*her bare arm. Why had she listened to Angelica Leone-Sterling, her friend and boss's wife, and purchased this strapless dress? It wasn't her, and it made her feel like someone she knew she couldn't be.*

His palm was rough and rasped her skin. Tingles spread up her arm and across her chest, making her nipples tighten against the lace of her strapless bra. She shivered and stepped away from his disturbing touch. He arched one eyebrow but made no comment.

"Yes," she said at last, knowing only that she needed to do something to take control of the situation before she forgot about her plans. Rand was a stepping-stone to the next level, she reminded herself.

"Shall we dance?" he asked again.

She nodded. His cologne—a spicy, masculine scent—surrounded her as they stepped onto the dance floor and he pulled her into his arms. *I'm in charge.*

But as his arms came around her and he settled her close against his chest, she didn't feel like she was in charge. She didn't want to be. Delicious sensations spread out from the hand he'd placed on the small of her back, radiating throughout her body and making her blood flow heavily through her veins.

She shuddered and tried to break the spell his touch was weaving by looking at him. But his eyes held a lambent gaze that pulled her further under his spell. The slow, sensual sounds of a jazz saxophone filled the room, and then the trio's lead singer, a tall black woman with a sultry voice, began to sing about wishing on a star.

Corrine had spent her entire childhood wishing for something that had never come. She thought she'd grown beyond that, but the temptation to rest her cheek on Rand's shoulder was strong and she knew she'd made a mistake. She had to get away.

She tugged free of Rand's grasp and hurried off the dance floor. What was with her tonight?

She headed for the bar and ordered a Stoli straight. She needed something to shock her back to her senses. Maybe she could blame this funky mood on the fact that her closest female friend, Angelica Leone-Sterling, had just announced she was pregnant.

Corrine knew she'd never have children. She wasn't ever going to do something as dicey as bring a child into this chaotic world. This world where nothing lasted forever and death came quickly and swiftly, taking no notice of those left behind.

Damn, she was getting maudlin. Maybe she shouldn't be drinking. But before she could rescind her drink order, she sensed Rand behind her.

"Make that two," he said to the bartender.

The bartender set the drinks in front of them. Rand paid for hers before she had a chance to get her money out.

"Here's some money for my drink," she said when the bartender moved away.

"I see that you are going to need some etiquette lessons as well as an escort for business functions."

"Why do you say that?" she asked. She knew she had manners. Mrs. Tanner, one of her foster mothers, had drilled manners into Corrine when she was eight years old. She didn't think she'd ever forget those lessons.

"Because you don't know how to say thank you. Put your money away."

She slipped the folded bill back into her beaded handbag. When you grew up on charity it was hard to accept a handout. And Rand wasn't her date for the night, he was a man she'd bid on. When she thought about it, maybe she should have paid for his drink. "I don't like to take advantage of people."

"I didn't think you were."

She took a sip of her drink, uncomfortable with the

silence that had fallen between them. The liquid burned going down, but she didn't flinch. Rand held his glass with a casual grace that made her feel awkward. She put her glass on a passing waiter's tray and noticed that he did the same.

"What happened on the dance floor?" he asked at last.

She shrugged. No way was she going to tell him that he'd taken her by surprise. That the rich boy who liked to win had needled his way past the barrier she thought would keep her safe from any man. "I just didn't feel like dancing."

He arched one eyebrow at her again.

"That's the most condescending thing I've ever seen anyone do," she said.

"What?"

"That lord-of-the-manor eyebrow thing you do."

He did it again. "It bothers you?"

"I just said so."

"Good," he said, caressing her cheek with his fingers.

"Why good?" she asked, trying to keep her mind off the shivers spreading over her body.

"Because you seem too removed from life."

"I'm in control. Something you should appreciate."

"I do. It's just fun to needle you out of your comfort zone."

"Rand, if we are going to have even a slim chance of getting along for our three 'dates' you are going to have to remember one thing."

"What's that?" he asked. Putting his hand on her elbow, he moved them out of the traffic path near the bar.

She waited until she was sure she had his attention. "I'm in charge."

"Where did you get that idea?"

"I don't know for sure, but I suspect it was when I wrote out the check to buy you."

"Did you say *buy me?*" he asked.

"Do you have a hearing problem? I might have to trade you in."

"You're playing with fire, Cori."

Why did he have to call her by that ridiculous nickname? No one had ever given her a nickname. In her first foster home they'd called her Corrine Jane. After that she'd made sure no one knew she had a middle name. When he called her Cori it was as if he was seeing inside her soul to the lonely little girl she'd been. And she didn't like that.

"I know how to keep from getting burned," she said carefully. Though with Rand she wasn't sure of anything. They'd known each other casually for almost a year, and she still felt uncomfortable when she was near him.

"How?"

She looked straight into those devastating eyes of his. Why had she started this? There was no way out of this, and she knew she had to retreat now before she did something really foolish and tell him she was afraid of the fire in his eyes.

"Stay away from the fire," she said, and turned to walk away.

"What if the fire doesn't stay away from you?" he asked.

She pretended not to hear him and continued across the ballroom to her table. She told herself she hadn't just issued a challenge to Rand but knew she had, and a part of her tingled in anticipation of what he'd do next.

Rand knew better than to follow her. A crazy kind of excitement buzzed through his veins. This was the first time a woman had inspired the feeling, and he wasn't sure how to handle it. The logic part of his brain said that Corrine was a woman and a client and he should leave it at that, but deeper instincts called for him to probe deeper into her psyche until she had no secrets left. Nowhere to hide from him.

He detoured by his partner's table. Angelica Leone-Sterling had the glow typical of a newlywed. More surprising to Rand, her husband, Paul, shared that same luminescence. Though they were both involved in separate conversations, Rand noticed their joined hands on the table.

For a moment he felt a pang at the loneliness of his life. Despite having four sisters and two loving parents. It was the same feeling that had dogged him since he was sixteen and a car accident had changed his life when his twin had died. But he'd learned to live with that missing part of himself. And until tonight he hadn't realized that he wasn't really living with it, rather just ignoring it.

He didn't want to examine it now. He had to settle for flirty banter instead of meaningful conversation with the opposite sex. But then he knew that everything in life was a trade-off.

He was a successful businessman. He had a trust fund most people only dreamed of. And on most days that was enough. But tonight wasn't one of them. Tonight his personal demon was rearing its ugly head and Rand fought to keep his jovial attitude. He really wanted to escape back to his dark corner of the world and go numb until he could escape.

He never should have followed Corrine to the bar and joined her for a Stoli. He knew better than to dance with a woman he wanted so badly that her perfume seemed etched in his memory, and her scent filled his every breath.

His reactions to Corrine weren't helping, either. He could still feel her in his arms, dammit. She'd fit perfectly, and he'd wanted to nudge her head onto his shoulder and keep her cradled there all night long.

That woman needed someone to cradle her, even though she'd never admit it. Unfortunately, he couldn't be that someone. The vow he'd made when he was twenty-one prevented him from being any woman's ''forever'' man, yet he wanted to remind Corrine Martin she was a woman. There was something in her cool gray eyes that made him want to shake her up.

She's a client, he reminded himself. ''Never let the

client get personal" was his mantra, but he wasn't behaving true to form tonight. He blamed it on the fact that he'd been conned into going on stage at this charity event when he'd sworn never to do so.

The problem was he'd never been able to resist a challenge. He wasn't sure when it had started, but he could remember having his first broken arm at age six when his older cousin Thomas had dared him to climb a tree. At thirty-five, he should be old enough to know better, but he liked the thrill he got from riding the edge of a dare.

It was a Super Bowl wager that had led to his participation in the themed "Buy a Bride" charity auction. Though he hadn't been the only man on the stage, it was still humiliating to participate in such an event.

Angelica looked up as he approached and smiled at him. She'd changed a lot since her second marriage last year. She was happier and more willing to take a chance. Their friendship had started with her first marriage to Rand's best friend, Roger. He and Roger had been roommates at military school and then in college. They had been closer than brothers.

Rand approached the table and made small talk until the right moment presented itself. He wanted a few minutes alone with Angelica.

"Want to dance?" he asked her, needing to talk to her without her husband around. Also, he needed to erase the memory of Corrine Martin in his arms.

"I don't know. Your technique must be off. I saw Corrine leave you earlier."

Great. He'd forgotten they were in a virtual fishbowl at these events. Usually he liked the attention and the feel of eyes on him. But when he'd held Corrine in his arms he'd forgotten all about being on display and had immersed himself in the sensations she elicited in him.

What was it with these women tonight? "The answer I'm looking for is yes or no."

She sighed. He knew she'd probe into what had happened, and he should probably leave her sitting at the table with her husband. But he needed to talk to his best friend and congratulate her on the pregnancy she'd just announced. He wanted to warn her about life and how one had to be cautious when you got close to having it all.

He'd have to be on his guard around Angelica. Watch over her at work and make sure that she stayed safe for Paul and the baby. He owed Roger that much—after all, Roger had saved his life. He felt a little more pressure tightening the back of his neck.

"Yes. I think they're playing our song," she said.

The band had begun to play "I've Got a Crush on You." It was the song they'd danced to at her first wedding so long ago. And over the years that song had helped them survive. Rand had held Angelica while she cried to that song on the anniversary of her first wedding.

There'd never been anything sexual between them; instead, she'd become like a sister to him. Though his own sisters would describe him as cold, he and Angelica had a warm relationship. Rand knew that was because of his debt to Roger.

Roger had guarded Rand's secret addiction and pulled him back from the edge. He owed Roger at first. Then he'd come to know and care for Angelica.

Rand knew a moment's fear for Paul and Angelica. It seemed as if they had too much. Rand had a healthy respect for the balance of the universe and the fact that you couldn't have it all. He prayed that Paul and Angelica would be the exception to that rule.

"Congratulations on your pregnancy," he said as they danced around the floor. They'd been partners in Corporate Spouses for more than ten years and friends even longer. Things were getting back to normal now. The tension at the back of his neck eased.

"Thank you. I'm a little nervous about it."

Her confession robbed him of the advice he'd been about to give. He couldn't tell her that fate never let anyone have it all. Because Angelica already knew that.

"I'll make sure you have everything you need, kiddo," he said.

"Oh, Rand. Thanks, but I think that's Paul's job now."

He swallowed, realizing it was true. The one woman he'd allowed himself to care about belonged to someone else now. That's good, he thought. Really, it is.

He tried to think of something else to say when he noticed one of the Tarron vice presidents, Mark something, escorting Corrine onto the dance floor. He didn't like how low the guy's hands were on Corrine's hips.

He maneuvered himself closer to the couple. Corrine's gaze met his and she seemed to want something from him. He looked closer at Mark and realized the man was drunk. Rand knew better than anyone how too many drinks could change the world around a man.

"Kiddo, you feel like using your power as the CEO's wife?" he asked Angelica.

"How?"

"I'm going to cut in and rescue Corrine from a man who's had one too many."

"I get to dance with a drunk. Boy, Rand, you sure know how to show a girl a good time."

"As you just pointed out, that's not my job anymore."

"You're right. Who is it?"

"Mark something, I think." He turned them so Angelica could see the man.

"Mark Jameson. His wife left him on New Year's Day—what with it being Valentine's Day—he hasn't been the same since then."

"Can you handle him?"

"No problem."

Rand spun them neatly into Mark and Corrine's path and tapped the other man on his shoulder. "May I?"

Mark's eyes were blurry and he looked a little confused. Angelica stepped into his arms as Rand tugged Corrine free. He heard Angelica use her most soothing voice as she took the lead in the dance and moved Mark to the edge of the dance floor.

"Thanks. I owe you one," Corrine said.

"I think I'll collect now," he said, even though he knew he should be escorting her off the dance floor and then collecting his keys from the valet and heading home.

"What do you want?"

That was a loaded question. "Don't walk away again."

She glanced up, obviously startled. "Ego problems?"

"Do you think I'm that shallow?"

"Yes," she said.

He laughed. There was a part of him that was shallow, and he did his best to make sure that was the only thing people saw.

"Maybe I just wanted to hold you for the three minutes or so that the song lasts."

"Don't say things like that."

"It's the truth." God, he wished it weren't, but his body had already decided that there was no way Corrine was going to be a hands-off client. She called to parts of him that he'd put away a long time ago. Nothing was going to be normal until he'd mussed up her cool exterior. Until he had her blond hair spread out on his pillow and was buried deep in her sweet body with her legs and arms wrapped around him.

"We have a working relationship, Rand. It can't be anything else."

"I'm aware of that," he said. He'd been working

with Corrine on the new training module he and Corrine were developing at Tarron.

"Why'd you bid on me tonight?" he asked. It was out of character for the woman he knew her to be. She'd given not only him but most of her co-workers the cold shoulder. She was cordial and polite, but she kept a distance between herself and others. The only person he knew who'd gotten past her barrier was Angelica. But then, Angelica had a way with people.

"You looked lonely up there."

He stopped dancing and glanced down at her. This was the second time she'd sassed him tonight. "Are you saying pity motivated you?"

"Well…yes."

"Darling, I seem to remember a brisk bidding before you finally won me."

"Cling to that memory," she said with a laugh.

He joined her, even though she was having fun at his expense. There was something warm and almost adorable in her eyes that made him want to protect her. Much the same as he'd wanted to earlier when he'd realized she was trapped on the dance floor. But he'd never been anyone's protector except Angelica's. And she'd been safe because Rand couldn't really fall in love with her. And he'd been doing it to pay back a debt. Business was the one thing he'd always been good at.

He was a loner by nature and he didn't want to get too involved with Corrine. He let his arms drop, and the music ended a second later. There was confusion in her eyes. He knew he had to get away before he gave in to the temptation to take everything she had to offer. Because the woman he'd just held had a softness that she didn't usually let the world see.

And that softness called to everything masculine in him. Made his chest swell and his muscles flex. It made him want to defend and protect her from everyone except himself. And Rand Pearson was no woman's hero.

He'd learned that the hard way.

He pivoted to leave.

"Is this payback?" she asked.

He stopped and took her elbow to escort her off the dance floor. He'd never forgotten his manners before. He prided himself on always being a gentleman. Something his parents had instilled in him since he'd first known the difference between boys and girls.

He stopped at the edge of the dance floor and turned to thank her for the dance. But those gray eyes of hers made the words die unsaid.

"I'm sorry," he said.

He walked away from her, knowing that he was going to need more than the words "never let the client get personal" help him this time. Because there was something about Corrine Martin that made him want to forget rules and lessons learned in life. And he was old enough to know better.

Two

Corrine neatly managed to avoid spending time with Rand until her first official date. She'd even corresponded with him through e-mail instead of calling him. His last e-mail had been brief to the point of seeming curt, but that didn't bother her. She regretted the impulse that had led her to bid on him and wished that she had some way to go back in time and change things. Although she knew that time travel didn't exist, she wished she could go further back than Rand Pearson's appearance in her life and make some huge alterations.

Today was a sunny Saturday in March, and Paul Sterling, Tarron's CEO, was having his annual staff party on his yacht moored in West Palm Beach. It was a two-hour drive from Orlando and Rand was picking her up.

She'd suggested meeting him there, but he'd sent back a reply saying only that he'd pick her up at ten. He pulled up at five till, and as he climbed out of his car and came toward her front door she wished again she'd never bid on him. Her pulse hammered, and everything feminine in her came to life.

She didn't have time for this. She'd wanted to have an escort to social functions because she always seemed to be the only one alone. And it made her stand out. She hated to have attention drawn to her. She liked blending in with the background.

She knew there was no way she was going to survive the two-hour drive down the coast unless she had a distraction. The doorbell rang and she glanced frantically around her neat house. Spotting her laptop in the corner she grabbed it and her leather carryall and headed for the door. Work had been her salvation since she was fourteen. She realized early that at work it didn't matter where you came from, only how well you did the job.

She shoved her Ann Taylor sunglasses up her nose and opened the door. The classic designer appealed to Corrine. Rand was leaning negligently against the porch railing, staring out at the street. She lived on Kaley, in one of Orlando's older sections. Her home had been built in the fifties and required lots of care, but she loved it.

"Nice neighborhood," he said, glancing up and

down the street, which wasn't too busy this Saturday morning.

"Thanks. Ready to go?" she asked, not wanting to encourage him to be nice to her. The other night had shown her that he'd slipped between her defenses and that was something she refused to let happen again.

"What, no tour?"

"Not today. I don't want to be late."

"We won't be. We've got five minutes to spare."

"Traffic could be heavy. I don't share your confidence."

"Want to bet on it?" he asked.

She knew from Angelica that Rand would bet on anything. And he usually won. She'd never gambled in her entire life. Not even on the twice-weekly Florida lottery. She preferred the safety of investing her money over the risk of losing a dollar to a chance of becoming a millionaire. "No."

"Scared?" His eyebrow rose behind his sunglasses.

"Of a bet with you? I don't think so."

"Then, why not?"

There was only way to beat this man, she thought. And that was with wit, because he was too smart and confident for his own good. "You don't really have anything I want."

He pulled his glasses down to the tip of his nose and regarded her over the top of the lenses. "Really?"

"Really," she said.

"I'll take that as a challenge."

She pushed her glasses back on her head and gave him her haughtiest stare. The one that made people back off. "Will your swelled head fit in the car?"

"No problem. The car is a convertible. I'll put the top down if need be."

She laughed and closed her door, locking it behind her.

"Why are you bringing your computer?" he asked.

"I have some work I need to do. I hate to waste the time since you're driving."

"You can't take one day off?" he asked.

"Sure I can. I just don't want to."

"Don't you ever have any fun?" he asked, opening her door for her.

"I like working."

She knew it was an old-fashioned gesture, and yet she liked it. He probably did it without thinking, but it made her feel good. She dropped her bags on the floor and smoothed the skirt of her sundress under her as she slid into the car. She felt the heat of his gaze on her legs as the hem slid up on her thighs.

Was he interested in her as a woman? Since he'd kept his distance after their dance she figured his attraction to her had been posturing since she'd been the one in the position of power.

He slammed the door and walked around in front of the car. He wore khaki shorts and a golf shirt and looked like an advertisement for easy living. She pulled her sunglasses back into place, then smoothed her hair along her head, searching for any strand that might have escaped the ponytail she'd pulled it into this morning. Neat and tidy, she thought.

"I like my job, too, but that doesn't mean I don't take time to enjoy life."

"I'm not an unhappy person, Rand. And you're working today."

"I know."

"So why shouldn't I?"

"Never mind."

She pulled her laptop from its case and powered it up. Rand fastened his seat belt and neatly backed out of her driveway. The traffic was heavy, but he wove through it effortlessly. She pulled up the company memo template and pretended to be composing the memo in her head, but all she could concentrate on was Rand.

His muscles flexed each time he shifted the car. She could practically smell the testosterone as he drove. And she wondered if she'd really survive if he decided to take her words as a challenge.

Because without even trying to, he was engaging her senses and distracting her from her work. She knew then that she'd never claim the other two dates she'd purchased from his company because there was no way she was going to be this close to him again after today.

Rand knew it shouldn't matter that she was working as they drove down to West Palm Beach. Ivanna Marckey, the last client he'd provided a corporate escort for, had spent all the time to and from engagements on the phone or reading e-mail on her PDA. But for some reason it bothered him when Corrine did the same.

That wasn't true. Not only did her actions disturb him—she did. From the tips of her hot-pink toes to her sleek blond ponytail. She seemed aloof and he wanted to bring her down to his level. He wanted to see her hot and mussed. He lowered the windows so the air circulated around them, tugging the long blond strands from her neat coiffure.

She glanced over at him. He knew he should have asked before he lowered the windows. He'd been raised with more manners than most, and this was one of the reasons why he'd left Chicago many years ago. He sometimes reacted without thinking. Something that Pearsons simply didn't do. Especially ones who seemed to live a charmed life.

"Do you mind?" he asked at last.

She shrugged. "I guess not. I wish I'd brought a scarf."

She turned back to her computer and started typing again. Obviously not too concerned with the wind. Or too ruffled by it.

"We'll stop before we get to the yacht club so you can fix your hair," he said, trying to make up for his behavior.

"Okay," she said. Her pleasantness made him feel like a bully on the playground.

He wanted to push harder to see what it would take to get a reaction out of her. A few more miles passed, and when they got on I-95 heading south he couldn't stand the silence anymore. It just left his mind free to wander and he'd never been that comfortable with himself. Usually he blared the radio on a heavy-metal station, but today there was an interesting distraction right next to him.

Her sundress was demure on the outside, but it was encasing a body that was his version of heaven. Long, slim limbs and generous curves above and below the waist. In his mind's eye he could still see her white thigh from when she'd gotten into the car.

He imagined his hand sliding up that leg. He knew it would be as smooth as silk. He'd touched her arms and shoulders the night they'd danced together and his fingers still remembered her texture. The roughness of his callused hands on her soft skin. He wanted to touch her again. Now.

Sexual tension pumped through his body, **making** him heavy. Dammit, he needed a diversion. **Too bad** she was engrossed in her job.

Which he knew shouldn't bother him, but it did. Everything male in him wanted to rise to the indirect challenge she issued by ignoring him. And that **was** the one thing he'd never been able to resist. **So he** fiddled with the radio dial until he found a **classic-**rock station.

Instead of something hard and raunchy, the sensuous sounds of Dave Matthews and his band singing one of their ballads. The soft, emotional lyrics didn't help his situation as he felt the beast in him rising to the surface.

He tightened his hands on the wheel. She hadn't

even glanced at him when the music blared out of the speakers. Unable to help himself, he reached over and removed the elastic holding her hair back. She didn't move to stop him, only glanced toward him.

"Problem?"

"You're going to have to take it out later, anyway," he said. Which had to be the lamest excuse in history. But there was no way he was going to tell her more.

She held her hand out palm up, and though he wanted to toss the damn elastic out the window he gave it to her. "Thanks," she said quietly.

"For what?"

"I put vanity before comfort."

"I don't imagine you being vain."

"Well, not like ego. I just like to look...well kept."

"I'll keep you well," he said before he could stop himself. Damn, normally he wasn't such a hound, but he could think of nothing but her in his arms. Her in his bed. Her...just her, and that disturbed him.

"Rand?"

"Don't, okay?" Rand asked.

He concentrated on the road. Hardly noticed that the long, sunshine-colored strands of her hair brushed his arm every thirty seconds or so. Hardly noticed that her scent engulfed him. He wanted to bring her closer so he could breathe her in. Hardly noticed that for once a different kind of tension was pursuing him.

He felt like a big, mean bastard. He turned the radio down and concentrated on his driving, annoyed at her for ignoring him and mad at himself for reacting as if he were in junior high school.

He clicked off the radio and floored the accelerator.

"You okay?" Corrine asked.

He'd had enough of being a beast and wasn't about to say another thing to her until they arrived at the yacht. And then he'd find a way to make sure he didn't take her actions so personally. But she appealed to him on too many levels. "Yeah."

She closed her laptop and put it away. "I've always loved the smell of the beach."

"Me, too. One of the first times I beat my older twin brother was at beach volleyball. We played all afternoon and we kept switching off winning, and then finally I won two in a row," he said.

"You know, I grew up in Florida but never got to go to the beach until I was in college. That trip was my shot at freedom, and I stood on the shore looking out at the endless horizon and vowed to make the most of every opportunity given to me."

"You've kept that vow," he said.

"Yes, I have."

"Why is success so important to you?" he asked. He knew that he shouldn't get to know her better. That knowing the woman behind the executive would only make her more tempting, but there was no way he could resist learning more about her. And the few glimpses he'd had of the real Corrine told him they weren't well suited. There was a sadness in her eyes sometimes that made him believe she needed an av-

erage guy without the baggage he brought to any relationship.

"I'm an orphan."

Her words didn't make sense to him at first. He
had so much family that he couldn't imagine a life
without them. And even when his five siblings
weren't around he had friends who were like family.
"When did your parents die?"

"I'm pretty sure they are both still living somewhere."

"Have you ever tried to find them?" he asked. He
liked knowing he was part of the past as well as the
future through his ancestry. Though he and his father
had never seen eye to eye on one thing, Rand
wouldn't change his lineage. He liked knowing where
he came from, and if the pressure of being a Pearson
was too much to bear sometimes, that was a price
Rand paid.

"No."

"You should think about it," he said.

"Rand, I'm never going to look for them."

"Why not?"

"I was abandoned when I was two days old."

Her words cut him. No one should have abandoned
this woman. Why hadn't he let her alone? "I'm
sorry."

"Why? It was a long time ago."

He reached across the gearshift and found her hand.
It was clenched in a tight fist, nails digging into the
flesh of her palm. Though her words sounded as if
she'd gotten over it, the truth was her emotions ran

deep and strong. He pried her fingers open and slid his hand around hers. And he knew how time could lessen the pain but not totally abate it.

He said nothing else as they drove along the highway, the wind in their hair and hands tightly clasped. She didn't speak, either, and when he pulled off the highway and had to let go to downshift, she reached for her handbag and pulled out a brush.

He knew he wouldn't be holding her hand again or seeing any more glimpses into her soul. Because as she put up her window, and he did the same, she morphed into someone he didn't want her to be. She smoothed her hair back into place, and she was no longer the woman he'd spoken to earlier but the corporate executive looking for her next promotion.

The party was fun in spite of being a work event. Corrine mingled through the crowd with Rand at her side. Tarron and Corporate Spouses had a strategic partnership for training—the project Rand and Corrine had been working on, so he knew many of her colleagues. As they circulated through the room, Corrine couldn't help being aware that this was how things might be if she ever had a husband. It was a little unnerving. Finally the party wound down and everyone started to leave.

"That went well," Corrine said as they helped tidy up after the party. Corporate Spouses had helped man the check-in table and had arranged for a caterer. Though Rand wasn't in charge of this event, he'd still made sure everything ran smoothly. And when Paul had asked her if she'd mind helping supervise the cleanup, Rand had said he didn't mind staying.

"Did it?" Rand asked.

He'd been distant since their conversation in the car and Corrine wasn't sure what to make of that. There was something about telling people that your own parents thought you weren't worth keeping that made them treat you differently. She'd revealed too much and had worked hard to keep him at arm's length during the luncheon. She shrugged. "I guess not."

He faced her suddenly, his green eyes intent. "It wasn't anything spectacular."

"Spectacular isn't necessary for success," she said.

"No, but it makes life more exciting."

She watched him working and realized that he craved excitement. It clung to him like a second skin. She knew then that if she hadn't bid on him they'd never have been intimate because they were in two totally different universes. Maybe they'd never been meant to meet. Every time she'd messed with fate it came back to haunt her. Just once she'd like to find a guy and have the kind of relationship that her peers at work seemed to take for granted.

"I like to blend in," she said.

He came over to her. The sun streaming through the windows behind him made it impossible for her to see his features. He touched her cheek, rubbing one finger down the length of her face, resting his hand against her neck.

"I noticed," he said.

She couldn't think while he touched her. She knew her pulse had increased. He probably felt her racing heartbeat. Could he see inside her? Did he realize that she wanted more from him than three cold impersonal dates? She stepped back. *I'm in control,* she reminded herself.

She felt like she should apologize but didn't. Quiet was who she was. "That's not your way, is it?"

"Not really. I like to shake things up."

"I noticed. I'm sorry I didn't want to play in that trivia game," Corrine stated, referring to the game many of the guests had played.

"No problem. I just thought we could win." She knew they would have. She'd always been good at those kinds of games but never played them in public. It seemed like the only people who participated at company events were the glory hounds and those who'd had too many drinks.

She had a strict rule about alcohol and work-related functions. She thought Rand must, too, because he'd drunk cola all day like herself. Actually, she'd drunk diet, but Rand didn't need calorie-free drinks. His body had been sculpted by years of being top dog. Of honing his body and skills until he was simply the best man in any room. Realizing an uncomfortable silence had fallen, she attempted to break the mood.

"Sometimes winning isn't the most important thing."

He grabbed his chest and staggered backward. "Say it isn't so."

Corrine chuckled. She liked his self-deprecating

humor. She liked that he'd let her set the tone for their presence at the party. She just plain liked him and that was…dangerous.

"What's wrong with him?" Paul asked from the other side of the room.

"I shocked him," Corrine said.

"How?" Paul asked.

"I told him winning wasn't everything," she said with a grin.

"Oh, no."

"Are you still weakened from the blow?" Paul asked Rand.

"Yes. That's my Kryptonite. Need a quick fix. Must win." Rand staggered around the room like a weakened man, clutching the table for support.

"Good. How about a quick match of beach volley-ball?" Paul asked.

Rand straightened slowly. "What did you have in mind?"

"Two on two. You and Corrine against me and Angelica."

Paul was looking at Rand, but Rand looked at her and Corrine wasn't sure what to do. She shrugged. "I don't have a change of clothes."

"Angelica keeps spare clothes on the yacht. I know she'd loan you some. I'll go check with her," Paul said, leaving the room.

She sensed Rand's eyes on her as she finished clearing the last table and put some things in the trash. She didn't want to look at him. Didn't want to see that challenging light in his eyes. But she glanced over her shoulder and was captivated.

"Wanna play?"

No, she thought. She wanted to retreat to her home ground—her safety area—and forget about her job and men and everything. At least until Monday when life would be normal again.

"I'm not good at sports," she said carefully. She prided herself on mastering whatever she attempted. When her prowess at sports never developed she'd given up on them.

"You said winning wasn't everything."

"But to you it is."

"How about we just have fun?"

"I can do fun."

"Really, without your laptop?"

"Make up your mind. Do you want me to play or not?"

"I want you to play, but it's up to you," he said.

She knew he'd be disappointed if she didn't play. Why did pleasing him matter? But for some reason it did. Before she could answer, Paul returned with Angelica.

"Come on, Corrine. It'll be fun," Angelica said.

Corrine nodded and found herself in a very short time standing barefoot in the sand wearing borrowed clothes. Rand wrapped his arm around her and pulled her close.

Her mind ceased functioning and all she could do was breathe in the masculine scent of his aftershave and feel the warmth of his body pressed to hers. His leg was hairy and tickled where it rubbed against hers.

"Here's the plan," he said, his words brushing across her skin.

"I can't hit the ball very hard," she said.

He smiled at her. It was the kind of smile that people always gave you when you were athletically challenged. "Don't worry. I can."

"Tell me what to do."

"I will."

"Don't let this go to your head," she said.

"How?"

"I'm still in charge."

"How can I forget it? You bought me, remember?" he asked.

She knew she didn't want to like him but realized it was too late. He served the ball and the game progressed. She realized that Rand Pearson was the kind of guy that made her wish she still believed in happy endings.

Three

Rand knew Paul had meant for the game to be friendly; the inclusion of the women pretty much said it without words. Angelica, though, was a fierce competitor and Corrine as well rose to the occasion, playing with more spirit than skill. But Rand had never been able to participate in any match and not give it his total concentration.

Even his demons demanded perfection from him. He did everything to the max without worry for the consequences. And sometimes the price he paid was high.

He forgot about winning the first time Corrine flinched, putting her hands up to block the ball instead of hitting it back over the net. But it soon became apparent that Corrine didn't like to be unsuccessful.

She watched Angelica and Paul and found weaknesses in their game that allowed her and Rand to stay even with them.

They'd probably be able to win if he could keep his eyes off her bare legs. It wasn't as if hers were the first he'd ever seen. But for some reason his eyes kept straying there. And his libido went into overdrive.

The sand was warm beneath his feet and he imagined only the two of them remained on the volleyball court. She was sweaty from the sun and from playing. Her T-shirt clung to her torso like a second skin, revealing all that her neat dress had hidden earlier. He wanted to toss the ball to the ground and pull her close to him. Not to huddle over game strategy but to taste those full lips of hers.

"Rand?" she asked. He imagined her calling his name in a much more intimate situation. Urging him closer to her body, bringing her mouth to his and whispering his name as her lips touched his.

"Rand?"

He glanced up to find Corrine staring at him. He became aware of the ball in his hands and the fact that he was supposed to be serving instead of ogling his teammate's legs. Damn, she got to him faster than any other woman he'd ever known. The tension that was always his companion settled in the pit of his stomach. It had been a long time since another person had affected him this deeply.

"Yes?" he asked, hoping his reaction to Corrine wasn't visible to the world. His beach shorts weren't made to disguise the hardening of his groin. He shifted a little and decided he had to concentrate on the game. The sexual thing he could handle if that were the only draw to Corrine. But the depths he kept glimpsing of this woman's soul made him wary.

"You okay?" she asked. She'd pushed her sunglasses to her head, and her eyes were serious as she watched him.

Did she suspect where his mind had been? "Fine. I was figuring out the score."

"Two-two," she said.

Okay, time to play and forget about the tempting woman whom he didn't want to like. The woman who'd shared some of her past with him and whom he realized he wanted to know more about. But he'd never ask. Because knowing more meant forming bonds and commitments. He wasn't a "forever" kind of guy. He couldn't ask anyone to share the life he lived because it was based on subterfuge.

He served the ball and the game ensued. It was fast and furious, and despite her claim not to be good at sports, Corrine played well. The next serve would determine who won the game.

Rand just couldn't wait for it to be over so he could hit the shower, preferably a cold one. And try to forget about how Corrine's shorts had ridden up on the curve of her buttocks as she'd lunged for the ball. She had a sweet, curvy rear that made his fingers tingle with the need to test the resilience of those curves.

"Time out," Corrine called, and walked to the center of the court. She stood there staring at him. Had she realized his mind wasn't on the game?

"You tired?" he asked. She was flushed and her eyes seemed exhausted.

She shook her head. "I want to talk to you."

He waited, but she gestured impatiently for him to join her. Angelica and Paul were huddled together, but it looked as if they were smooching rather than discussing strategy. Part of him hungered for what they had, but Rand quickly pushed it deep down and ignored it as he always did. Having it all came at a high cost and he wasn't willing to pay the price.

"What's up?" he asked.

"Umm…"

He waited. She didn't smell sweaty, he realized, but faintly floral and something else that he associated only with Corrine. He'd held her in his arms twice and some things had become imbedded in his senses.

"Were you serious about playing for fun?" she said at last.

Not really, but he knew that coaxing her into the game had been his motivation earlier. Still, he couldn't tell her how important winning was to him. "Yes, why?"

"Good." She nibbled her lower lip and he watched. He thought she said something about not caring if they didn't win, but all he could do was watch her teeth and tongue and her sexy lips and wonder how they'd taste under his. Would she react with the passion he sensed was bottled up inside of her? Or would she be cool like her outer surface image?

"I think we have a good shot at winning," he said at last.

"What if we didn't?" she asked.

He realized she was trying to tell him something without saying the words. "I'm not making the connection here, darling. Just tell me what you're trying to say."

She shrugged. "I don't think I should beat my boss."

"Paul doesn't care if we win. I've played him lots of times at basketball and golf. I usually win," he said.

"That's different."

"How do you figure?" he asked, leaning closer to her.

She tilted her head to the side and then stood on her tiptoe to whisper in his ear. "You don't work for Paul."

He ignored the jolt of that went through him. "That's right, I don't."

She pulled back and met his gaze evenly. "You work for me, right?"

He arched one eyebrow. "We both know I do."

She grimaced at him. "I'd like to see you lose when you do that eyebrow thing."

"Oh, does it bother you?"

"You can be so annoying when you try."

"I know. It's a gift."

"I don't like it, Rand."

"I'll try to remember that."

"Good. Remember what else I said."

"You didn't say anything."

"Then I'll say it now. I'd rather not win."

"Do you have a plan to lose? Because Paul will notice if we suddenly start missing the ball."

"You'll just have to pretend to be distracted," she said.

"How am I supposed to do that?"

"You're a smart man. You'll think of something."

Several seconds passed before Rand replied to her rather provocative words. "Will you be distracting me?" he asked. There was something very masculine in his tone that made everything feminine in her stir. She wanted to run from Rand and the male gleam in his eyes but she was made of stronger stuff.

The cowardly part of her doubted that. But she was determined to stay where she was. "How?"

Her world was very narrow and she'd never had to distract a man before. Manipulate them a time or two in a business situation to get the results she wanted, but never distract. Her mind was going wild trying to figure out what he had in mind.

He muttered something under his breath. She tugged at the hem of the jogging shorts that Angelica had loaned her. They were shorter than she was used to, but otherwise fit well.

"What'd you say?" she asked.

"Nothing. You just stand there and I'll be distracted," he said.

It was the closest thing she'd ever had to a compliment from a man. Usually she froze them out before they could work up the nerve to say anything personal to her. She'd learned a long time ago that life was simpler without interpersonal relationships.

But there was something about Rand that made her not want to freeze him out. That made her want to try to bring him closer to her. That made her…just want him.

"Really?" she asked without thinking.

He gave her one of those lord-of-the-manor looks and she wished she'd kept her mouth closed. But it was too late. Besides, he was too arrogant for his own good.

"Don't pretend you don't know that you are an attractive woman," he said.

Scooting a few feet away from him, she glanced objectively down at her body. She spent some time working out so she wasn't overweight, but when she looked in the mirror all she saw was a rather average-looking woman. Now wasn't the time to argue the point with him, but she knew he was mistaken.

A change of subject was needed. "What if I just talk to you?"

"You haven't been quiet the entire game and that hasn't affected my playing," he said.

He was right. She didn't really know how to play the game and had been calling questions to him. He'd been really good and he was hard to distract. One time she'd yelled at him to watch out when he'd dived for the ball and he'd still managed to hit it over the net.

He was a superb athlete. He wore only surf shorts,

leaving his chest bare. He was tanned and his muscles were firm and delineated. She knew why she wanted to believe he found her attractive—he was the kind of man that she'd always secretly drooled over.

Actually, she should probably be the one to act distracted by him. Of course, it wouldn't be an act. She hadn't been able to keep her mind on work all day. Instead of being the key to her next promotion, Rand seemed more like her Achilles' heel.

"What if you think you see someone you know on the beach?" she said. This game needed to end, and soon. She wanted—no, needed—to be back at her small house spending another Saturday evening working on her computer or watching *The Scarlet Pimpernel* on video. No more time in the presence of this man.

"Corrine, if we have to explain what happened it'll look rigged. Trust me—if we win, Paul will still respect you."

"I don't want to do anything to jeopardize my position at Tarron," she said.

"How will this game affect your role there?" he asked.

Now that she had to explain it she felt a little silly. But the truth was there were people who looked down on her because she'd been Paul's secretary before being promoted to manager of operations. And telling Rand didn't devalue her. It only gave validity to the circumstances at work. "I have to be careful about the job, that's all."

"Why?"

"You know I was Paul's administrative assistant." He nodded.

"Some people think he gave me the job because I was displaced from being his secretary when he was promoted. He kept Tom's secretary, Jane."

"Then they don't know Paul or you. He'd never give you a job you couldn't do. And you'd never take one."

She wondered how he knew that about her. It was the nicest thing anyone had ever said about her. She wanted to hug him and hold his words close to her. "Thank you."

"You're welcome. What do you say we let fate decide this match?"

She was about to ask his opinion again, but then remembered that she steered the course to her destiny. And Rand was right. Any boss who'd be upset over losing a game of volleyball wasn't someone she'd be able to respect, and she'd always had the utmost respect for Paul Sterling.

"Okay," she said softly.

"Attagirl!" Rand said, chucking her under the chin.

"Could you try not to sound so patronizing?"

"I don't patronize you."

"*Attagirl?* You make me sound like a five-year-old."

"Baby, I definitely don't think of you as a kid. Stop being so defensive."

"I'm not." As soon as the words left her mouth she realized she sounded like a grade-schooler arguing.

"Are you two going to huddle all day?" Angelica called.

"No," Corrine said. Thankful for the distraction, she returned to her spot near the net.

"Ready, Cori?" Rand asked.

She nodded. Damn the man, he knew he was getting under her skin. She took her position, ready to play her best, and determined to keep Rand Pearson at arm's length no matter how much her instincts might want to draw him closer.

Rand knew he should back off, let Corrine set the tone for the last minutes of the game, but he didn't. Paul was watching the two of them and Rand knew what the other man was thinking. That somehow over the course of the game Corrine had become personal to him. Dammit. No woman got personal. He prided himself on it. His survival depended on it.

And they were winning the game—to hell with what she wanted. He wasn't her lapdog. The agreement they'd signed was one where he escorted her to social functions. This game was not inclusive. Paul had invited *him* to play.

But when he set up to serve and Corrine glanced over her shoulder at him, he knew she was nervous. She nibbled on her lower lip and he felt his resolve crumble. Maybe those feelings went back to when his twin, Charles, had asked Rand to get in the car with him when they'd been sixteen. Maybe it went back to his first summer job at his dad's firm. He hated to disappoint anyone. Maybe it had to do with cheating death more than once and that feeling in his gut that if he didn't live right he might not get another chance.

He just couldn't do it.

So he served the ball straight to Angelica, knowing

she'd be able to lob it easily back over the net, which she did, right at Corrine. He'd left the game in her hands. She broke eye contact with him and jumped for the ball.

He knew she'd probably miss it. She hadn't hit all that many balls today and it would be a believable loss, but instead she tapped it on the outside and it came right at him.

Time seemed to move in slow-motion as the ball came toward him and Corrine's eyes met his. In them he read the same exhilaration he felt at the end of a close game. In them he read the determination to win. In them he saw a reflection of the woman who'd confessed to never being good at sports and wanting to be, this one time.

He leapt into the air and hit the ball with restrained power, this time sailing it over Angelica's head. Paul dove for the ball and barely missed it.

There was total silence. Rand wasn't sure he'd read the signs correctly. Did Corrine want to win? He'd done it for her, but would she believe that? He was almost afraid to look at Corrine and see whatever lurked in her eyes.

Women complicated a man's life, he acknowledged. And though the thrill he'd gotten watching her lithe body move on the sand had been nice, it wasn't worth this type of difficulty. He should have learned his lesson a long time ago and never agreed to this co-ed game. Men were more predictable about sports and winning.

He crossed slowly toward her. Angelica was grinning at Paul, who was covered in dirt and sweat. He was aware on a peripheral level that Angelica was comforting her husband on losing. But his main focus was the blond woman staring at him.

"We won," she said, her voice barely a whisper. She'd pushed her sunglasses back on her head and her gray eyes sparkled in the waning twilight. Eyes were supposed to be the windows to the soul but hers were guard posts, and he thought they did their job too well. He couldn't read a damned thing in them.

"We did," he said. He rarely lost and never tired of winning.

"I've never won at a sport."

"How's it feel?" he asked, still not able to gauge her mood.

She smiled then and his troubles should have melted away, but instead he felt a sense of doom. Because that smile was sweet and innocent and cut past the layers he used to keep others at bay. That smile made him want to always be her champion and he knew he wasn't going to be Corrine's.

"It feels incredible," she said.

"Good game," Paul said as he and Angelica ducked under the net to join them. Rand shook hands with the other man and hugged Angelica. Corrine did the same.

"Thanks." He tried to see if she was nervous but couldn't read her. Which was no surprise—she kept her true self carefully hidden.

"We got lucky there at the end." Though he knew it wasn't true. That last play had involved skill and precision. Maybe Paul wouldn't notice.

"Is that why you always win?" asked Paul.

"Not usually," Rand said wryly.

"Then I don't think luck deserves the credit. We're

going to clean up on the boat. See you at work on Monday, Corrine.''

Paul and Angelica walked away and Rand watched them go. "Sorry I couldn't convince Paul it was luck that brought us victory."

"That's okay."

The beach wasn't too crowded this late in the afternoon. Corrine moved away from him to the low wall that separated the court from the parking lot and sat on the ledge. He wondered what was going through her head.

"You okay?"

"Yes. It felt good to win."

"I never tire of it," he said, crossing to her. Sometimes he thought his interest in sports was the only thing keeping him sane. He stood a few feet from her and looked at her. She swung those long, shapely legs of hers back and forth. He could almost feel something in the air pulling him toward her.

"I might want to do it again."

Don't flirt, he warned himself, but his mind refused to listen. "With me?" he asked.

She shrugged. "Maybe."

"Maybe?"

"Maybe," she said again.

She was sassing him again and he liked it too much to walk away. "Ah, I see. I give you your first taste and you're going to leave me behind to sample it again."

"Would that bother you?" she asked.

He closed the gap between them, standing between her legs. She stopped swinging them and tilted her head back to look at him.

"If I said it did, would that matter to you?" he asked, not wanting to reveal too much to her.

He wondered if the rise in endorphins could be blamed on the flush of victory. But he knew that it was her close proximity that was responsible for the blood pooling in his groin and hardening him.

"Say it and see," she said. She licked her lips, and he knew that he wasn't standing there to flirt with her. He acknowledged that he'd moved in to taste those lips of hers. To feel that supple body of hers pressed to his.

He lowered his head slowly in case he'd read her wrong, but she didn't pull away. Instead, she cupped the back of his head and rose to meet him. Nothing had ever tasted sweeter than her mouth when it met his.

Nothing had ever tasted more forbidden, either, because her embrace was filled with both a woman's passion and a sweet shyness that could only be Corrine.

Four

Rand's body pressed against hers, surrounding her with his heat. He smelled earthy and sweaty, like a primal man calling to all the instincts she carefully hid beneath her wall of aloofness.

Shivers spread down her arms from where he held her. She opened her mouth wider, inviting him deeper. He thrust his tongue into her mouth with a surety that told her he knew his way around a woman's body. Later that might bother her, but right now she thanked God for it.

Her breasts felt heavy and full and she leaned forward until her torso rested against his. Her nipples started to tighten and she rotated her shoulder blades, brushing her aroused flesh against the rock-hard planes of his chest.

Rand groaned deep in his throat, his thumb idly caressing her neck as if he had all day to get to know her mouth. As if he'd stay where he was until he'd uncovered all the secrets there. As if he'd wait for her to be ready for more.

And for the first time in three years, Corrine was ready for more. *Much more.* She tugged him closer between her spread thighs.

She wasn't a virgin; she'd had sex before and occasionally enjoyed it, but Rand was shattering her illusions about what she wanted. Lust wasn't in her program.

She was focused on her job. Her career path had become more important to her than all those other relationships, but as he slid his hands down her back, cupping her backside and sliding her forward on the low wall until he rested at the notch of her thighs, she realized she didn't care.

All that mattered was this moment. Rand's large hands slipping over her back and under the hem of her shirt. The roughness of his calluses as he slid his hands down her spine. His long fingers dipping beneath the waistband of her shorts, caressing the furrow between her buttocks. She moaned in the back of her throat, realizing that she was never going to be able to get her guard up around him again.

His kisses were like a drug, making her crave them more and more. She ran her hands over his chest and pecs. Damn, he was in really good shape. His hips were wedged between her thighs and she felt as if she were on the cusp of something.

A piercing wolf whistle made Rand raise his head. Some beach bum was ogling them. His mouth was still wet from hers and she reached up, rubbing her thumb over his bottom lip. He nipped at her finger and tucked her head against his chest, holding her in a hug that made her realize there was more between them than a business contract and lust.

That thing felt scarily like caring. *Oh, God, don't let it be caring.* Caring was the one thing she'd always avoided. Or tried to avoid. She kept her feelings to herself, because every time she'd ventured out of her shell she'd been hurt badly. She wasn't taking that chance again. She had a plan for the future and she was going to work that plan and that plan only.

''That almost got out of hand,'' he said after a few minutes. He dropped a soft kiss against her temple and continued holding her in his protective embrace. No one had ever tried to protect her. She wasn't sure she liked it. Because she realized he knew she had vulnerabilities.

He was still hot and hard between her legs, and she regretted he'd kissed her in such a public place. They could have followed things to their natural conclusion if they'd been some place private. She could no longer pretend the attraction between them didn't exist.

Corrine regretted that.

''Yes, it did. Why?'' she asked.

He leaned back and gave her one of his lord-of-the-manor looks. She flushed.

"Hey, I'm blond. I think I'm allowed the occasionally ditzy comment."

"You know you're leaving yourself open to all kinds of jokes now."

"Isn't that a little too easy for you?" she asked. He smiled at her, and she realized that she liked the way he teased her.

"Where you're concerned there's no such thing as easy." There was a seriousness to his tone that belied the light moment. She realized that for all that she was trying to protect herself from getting hurt, Rand might be doing the same thing.

"If I'm that much trouble, why do you bother?" she asked. No one had ever thought she was worth the trouble. Not her mother or father, not the series of foster parents she grown up with, not the men she'd dated. Was Rand serious?

Grasping her face in his big hands, he tilted her head back and then kissed her. This time his restraint was marked, but fire still zipped through her body, making her nipples tighten and the flesh between her legs throb. He stepped back and lifted her down from the wall she was sitting on.

"You're worth it," he said, dropping his hands and walking away.

Corrine watched him go, aware that he'd crossed a line. And she realized as she slowly started after him toward the clubhouse to change that she didn't regret his boldness. In fact, she hoped he'd do it again… soon.

That thought scared her, because it meant that

she'd already started to drop her guard. There was a darkness in Rand's eyes that mirrored the one in her soul. And she didn't think ''casual'' was in the cards for them.

Rand emerged from the washroom to find Corrine waiting. The tepid shower he'd just taken had gone a long way to cooling him down, but one look at her and his blood immediately heated and the unresolved desire returned. He wanted her like he'd wanted no woman in the past.

And if she were a different kind of woman, he would take her. They had the weekend—normally that would be enough to assuage him. But he sensed with Corrine he'd want more. He'd need more. He'd never be pleased with anything less than the total annihilation of her cool outer facade.

And he also knew there was no way he'd be able to remain uninvolved if he slipped the leash of his control. Already the tension that was his daily companion was intensifying, making him shake with a weakness he refused to acknowledge.

Corrine Martin was dangerous. He didn't know why she made him react the way she did, only that she did. And he didn't like it. He wanted to blast through her icy exterior and make her the vulnerable one, not him—never again.

She looked fetching, standing there backlit from the setting sun, which streamed in the plate-glass windows. *Fetching* wasn't a word he usually used, but there was something about Corrine that brought out his old-fashioned notions of courting. Hell, she brought out the most old-fashioned thing between a man and a woman in him—lust.

It wasn't only that he'd tasted her mouth and felt the passion she kept tightly under control. She'd left her hair down. Damp from her shower but starting to dry, it brushed her shoulder and curled with a slight wave. He regretted he hadn't taken the time to touch her hair earlier. It looked like silk with the sun illuminating it, and he clenched his hands to keep from crossing to her and taking her head in his grip.

But he knew caressing her velvety hair wasn't going to be enough. He'd soon be tipping her head back and exploring her mouth until she rose to meet him. Until she became as overcome as he. Until nothing less than total completion would satisfy either one of them.

Yeah, he should've felt her hair earlier, but frankly, his body had been focused on much more responsive areas of hers. He'd been on overdrive and needed to arouse in her the same passion that had been flowing through his veins.

"Hi," she said softly. Her voice brushed over him like the hot sun had earlier, making him feel heavy and lethargic. His groin tightened a little more and he shifted his bag so that she wouldn't notice.

He nodded at her, unsure if he could talk right now. He was used to playing and winning, even with women. Winning made him feel in control and sure of himself. And there was a vulnerability in Corrine's eyes that warned this wasn't a game. Or at least not one that would leave behind a victor.

"Hi, yourself," he said, trying for a casualness he didn't feel.

His beast had slipped the civilized reins of his up-bringing and the veneer of sophistication was a mem-ory. Winning always brought him a rush, but holding a woman in his arms had never affected him the way Corrine had. Her taste was still on his lips, the feel of her skin, soft and smooth, was still under his fin-gertips, and the feel of her tightened nipples still abraded his chest.

He hardened more, undoing the effects of the shower. *Damn.* He hadn't counted on this. Hadn't counted on her or the way she made him forget the things about himself he'd always taken for granted. He'd had success with women for one reason and one reason only. He wasn't playing for keeps, so it was easy to play to win. Easy to put their needs first and make them feel as if they were the center of his world.

He knew with gut-deep sureness that if he made Corrine the center of his world—with her wide, un-guarded eyes and her shy smile—he'd never want to let her out of his life. And he wouldn't ask anyone to share the shadowy world that was his reality. He might have the world fooled into believing he was the easygoing owner of a successful business, but deep in the night, under the cover of darkness, he knew the truth.

"Ready to leave?" he asked, starting for the door.

Maybe if he could make it to the car and concentrate on driving, this would go away. *Yeah, right.*

"Um...Rand?"

He glanced over his shoulder at her. She hadn't moved. Her straw bag was still over her shoulder, but her hands were crossed around her waist in the most defensive position he'd ever seen.

She wrinkled her nose. "Thanks."

"For what?"

"Winning."

"No problem," he said.

"It isn't for you, but for me it usually is."

"Like you said, winning isn't everything."

"Maybe it's the adrenaline from taking a risk."

"Why risk?"

"I was unsure of Paul's reaction."

"Paul's a nice guy," Rand said. Why the hell were they talking about Paul?

"Yes, he is...nice."

Where was this inane conversation going? He dropped his bag and strode back to her, aware there was more she wanted from him than just a rehash of something that had happened earlier.

"What's with all this niceness?" he asked, barely an inch of space separating them.

"You don't think Paul is nice?"

"Cori, I'm hanging on to my control by a thread. At this moment Paul is the last person on my mind."

"Who's on your mind?"

"Do you really not know?"

She shrugged. "I don't know myself around you. I feel achy and I don't like it."

He framed her face in his hands and bent his head, taking her sweet mouth with his. She dropped her bag and wrapped her hands around his shoulders, holding him to her. He wasn't going anywhere. Not now. Not until he'd appeased the hunger deep inside him.

But not here, he thought. He needed to get them someplace with total privacy. And he needed to think. He lifted his head, rubbed his thumb across her lower lip. Her mouth was wide and full and meant to be under his. Rand dropped a few small, teasing caresses on her face and then stepped away, glancing at his watch.

He saw the uncertainty in her eyes and knew that if he didn't encourage her she'd retreat back behind that coolness she used to keep the world at bay. Deep inside he was touched. Hell, more than touched that she'd dropped her guard for him.

But he knew fate well. Knew that a man wasn't meant to have it all. A long time ago, Rand had decided wealth was enough for him. It wasn't as risky as emotion.

"Well, that was *nice*," he said.

"I'm ready to go home," she said, grabbing her straw bag and walking out of the clubhouse without another word. But each tattoo of her sandals echoed in the room, saying to Rand, "Bastard."

There wasn't anger in her steps, only disappointment, and he wasn't used to inspiring that kind of reaction in women.

* * *

Corrine prided herself on being a smart woman. She rarely had to be shown or told how to do something more than once. In fact, she'd received recognition at work for her quick thinking. So as she sat next to Rand, driving back to her house, she knew with absolute certainty that she would never again attempt to step outside her box.

She thought about pulling out her laptop and escaping into her work but knew that this time work wouldn't be the escape she needed. She had a slight sunburn from being outside, but that sensation didn't bother her as much as what had happened with Rand. Was it his reaction that made her feel this way or the fact that she'd wanted something more from him?

Something physical and deep. Something that wouldn't go away. Because even though she knew he didn't want her, because no one ever really had—but she still wanted him. Her pulse beat languidly and her skin was sensitized. She still felt him pressed along her body, and there was a part of her that wouldn't be content until he was touching her again.

But he didn't want to. He'd made it abundantly clear in one fell swoop. Had he glimpsed the thing that made her unlovable? She wrapped her arms around her waist, chilled at the thought that her vulnerability was so easily visible to this man. The one man who made her want to reach out to him saw her for the incomplete woman she was.

"Cold?" he asked.

She shook her head. Huddling deeper in her seat,

she glanced out the window at the passing landscape. She'd lived her entire life in Florida…carved out a safe niche for herself. And only today had she realized how cold and lonely her place in the sun was. The future suddenly took on a new meaning, and her career, which had been her focus for so long, paled when she thought of her elderly years spent alone with only her mind for company.

"Sure?" he asked after a few miles.

"Yes," she said firmly. It felt as if he was offering her an olive branch. Why the hell didn't she just take it?

But she couldn't. She'd spent her entire adult life keeping everyone at bay, and the one time she wanted to let someone closer—not just anyone, but Rand—he didn't want to come.

He fiddled with the radio, tuning into a hard-rock station. Music blared from the speakers and she wondered if he was trying to quiet his mind with the music. It wasn't working for her. His words echoed over and over in her mind, like a hunter circling his prey…*that was nice.*

Their embrace had shaken her moorings, making her question things in her life that she'd always taken for granted. The very fabric of who she was had ripped in half, and she realized she didn't know herself with this man. Why him?

What was it about Rand that made her sit up and take notice? Suddenly she couldn't wait another minute. She flicked off the radio and he turned to her. He glanced at her from beneath the dark rims of his sunglasses, but his eyes were not visible to her.

He raised one eyebrow at her in question. Unable to help herself she mimicked the action back to him. He cracked a grin but didn't say anything. She liked him, dammit. Why was it when she finally found a man she thought she could connect with he was all wrong for her?

"Did you want something?" he asked after a few minutes of silence.

"Yes." She wanted him. Even if it was only for a short-term affair. But how did you ask a man who you'd bought for business to suddenly make the arrangement personal?

"Why?" she asked at last.

"Why what?"

"I guess I meant, why not? Since the moment we met you've been flirting with me, and when I finally take you up on it..." She couldn't say it out loud. Even though she'd known her entire life that she was not a keeper she didn't want him to realize it. Except he already had.

It had started with her birth parents and followed her throughout her entire life. Quick learner that she was, you'd think she'd have caught on by now. But there was always a feeling of hope deep in her soul that maybe this time someone would want to keep her.

He cursed savagely under his breath, slowed the car and pulled off on the shoulder. He didn't look at her, but instead stared out of the windshield. Not saying a word to her, he rubbed his forehead.

"I got the feeling you didn't want more from me," he said at last.

He had her. Why was it she never seemed to realize how important a person was to her until he'd moved on? "Well, I didn't."

He shifted the car into Park and turned toward her in the seat. He laid his arm behind her, and though he didn't touch her she felt the heat of him. Something deep inside her let loose and she realized that even if she made a fool of herself, this man was important to her and she couldn't let him go without a fight. "So what's the problem?"

"I don't know. It's just that..."

"What?" he asked. He removed his sunglasses and those green eyes of his bore into her. She felt as if he was seeing past the conversation she was using to protect herself.

"It's been a long time since a man kissed me like you did," she said.

"Really?" he asked, his voice dropping to a low, husky growl. His hand moved to the back of her neck, rubbing in a slow, sensuous circle.

"God, I should've known better than to say that to you, ego man." His touch made it hard for her to think, but she didn't want him to stop. God, why was this man the one to bring her to aching attention? Why did he call to all that was feminine in her?

"It's not ego. You're a hard woman to read."

"I've lived a hard life," she said quietly. There

was no use hiding it from Rand. She wasn't the woman she tried to present to the outer world. Though she knew she'd keep up the image around him, he had to know there was more underneath the surface.

"I don't want to hurt you," he said, glancing away from her and taking his hand from her neck.

She wondered if she might already matter to him a little bit. It would be so easy to sink back into silence and let this conversation die, but she wasn't about to miss out on Rand. Something about him called to the wild, untamed part of her soul that she'd hidden forever. Taking his hand in hers, she said, "I won't let you."

"Nothing can stop fate." He turned his hand in her grasp so that he was the one holding her hand. His fingers were large, engulfing hers completely. His thumb rubbed over her knuckles and she knew he meant nothing sexual by his touch, but that didn't stop shivers from spreading up her arm.

"What do you mean?" she asked.

"Just that happiness is a delicate balancing act, and what we feel for each other is too explosive not to blow up in our faces."

She studied him for a moment. "Where does this leave us?"

"With a handful of firecrackers," he said.

She just waited, sensing that he had more to say. He sighed, brought her hand to his lips and kissed her. She felt like a maiden of old receiving a knight's colors. And for the first time since she met him she realized that Rand wasn't wearing shining armor and riding a grand steed. He was weary and riding a horse that had seen too much battle.

That glimpse shook her. There was more to this flirty playboy than she'd imagined. Sensing she wasn't the only one who could get hurt, she wanted to pull back, but he smiled at her.

"How about we start with dinner?" he asked.

Even though she knew better, knew that there was no way she was going to be able to keep this man at arm's length, she smiled and nodded. He drove them to Tasty Thai, where they ordered takeout, and then went to her house to eat it. All the while Corrine knew that she had taken a step that would change her life forever.

Five

Two hours later, Rand still wasn't sure he'd made the best decision, but he couldn't regret spending the evening with Corrine. Her house was neat and homey. Not what he'd expected from her all-business persona. He could tell that she'd created a sort of sanctuary for herself. The only thing missing were family photos. In fact, there were no photographs in the entire house. He'd taken a tour while she'd brewed some iced tea for them.

She'd offered him a beer with dinner, and for the first time in a long time, he'd been tempted to take it and drink it. Corrine made him feel things and he preferred to live in the safety of numbness. At social functions he usually held a glass in his hand and didn't taste it because one taste was never enough.

But tonight his control was shaky, and even smelling alcohol was something he didn't want to attempt. He hoped once he'd had Corrine in his bed, once he'd exorcised the passion she wrought effortlessly from him, he might be able to find his equilibrium again.

Her living room was a homage to the cinema, and it was clear to him that her secret passion was movies. Her bookshelves were crammed full of script versions of films and biographies of movie stars. She had a state-of-the-art home theater system that rivaled his own. As the evening had progressed he'd realized that Corrine might freeze everyone out at work and be a top-notch businesswoman, but the real woman underneath was a bit of an innocent.

There was a part of him that wanted to uncover all of her secrets. She'd teased and flirted with him throughout dinner, and now that they were in the living room enjoying coffee and the sounds of mellow jazz on her Bose speaker system, he should be relaxing.

But she was close to him on the couch. Her pheromones were doing too good a job at attracting him, and he felt as if he might fall on her like a hungry dog unless he distracted himself. No matter that she'd all but asked him to spend the night in her bed. He needed to remember that he'd made a vow to stop hurting the innocents of the world a long time ago.

"I can't believe you don't like period movies. *Emma* was one of the best I've ever seen."

"It's a girlie movie."

"Girlie movie? *Thelma and Louise* is a girlie movie."

"Point taken. Why did you think I'd like that?"

"You just seem different from other men," she said.

He wasn't sure how to take that. He was different and had been for a long time. "You think I'm girlie."

She swatted his shoulder. "Don't be obtuse."

"I'm not."

She gave him a very serious look, but there was a sparkle in her eyes. And he knew that she was teasing him. Suddenly it became very important that he handle her carefully. Because he realized that she was slowly blossoming here tonight. She'd started earlier at the beach when her focus had widened off of work, and then over dinner it had continued.

Normally he'd be happy that a woman he wanted showed signs of wanting him with the same intensity, but tonight, with the full moon shining in through her bay window and the sensual music pouring through the speakers, seduction no longer seemed the order of the day. Seduction, in fact, seemed a violation of the trust that was slowly building between them.

A trust that Rand knew to be false because he was hiding the truth of who he was from her.

"What's your favorite movie?" she asked.

"*Star Wars*."

"Good choice. The mythical story structure and impact on cinema alone make it a good choice."

"I was thinking of Princess Leia in her bondage outfit."

"You're into bondage?"

"Only if it excites you," he said. He'd like nothing better than to tie her to his bed.

She wrinkled her nose. "I don't think I'd like it."

"I promise you would," he said.

"Get that gleam out of your eyes. I was teasing you."

"I know," he said. He'd lived a decadent life in part because he'd been running from his image as the good son and also because when you had everything, life got boring. But he'd long ago given up on jading innocents.

There was a brief lull in the conversation and Corrine leaned her head back with her eyes closed. "You're the first person I've had to the house for dinner."

"Should I feel special?" he asked.

She turned her head and her bright gray eyes made him feel as if he were being measured. "Yes."

Oh, Corrine, he thought, don't feel too much. Unable to wait another minute, he reached out and touched her cheek. She shivered under his touch. And he knew that the electricity that he felt whenever they were together wasn't one-sided.

"Why do you keep people at arm's length?" he asked.

She shrugged. "It's just easier."

"Why?"

"Don't laugh," she said.

He tugged her close and hugged her tight. "Never."

"Everyone always leaves."

The words were spoken so softly he could barely hear them. And he wasn't sure he understood. But then he remembered her comment on the drive to the beach about her parents abandoning her.

"Like your parents?"

Her fingers nervously kneaded the fabric of his shorts where they covered his thigh. He knew she meant the touch to be impersonal, but he found it arousing just the same. He also knew now wasn't the time for lust.

"Yes," she said.

"How do you know they left you?"

"My foster mother told me."

"How old were you?"

"When she told me the truth?" He nodded. "Six."

"Why did she tell you?"

"I kept crying for my real parents every night, hoping they'd come and take me from the home."

He heard all she didn't say. That those words had cut her more deeply than any others could. He tightened his arms around her. Holding her closer, wishing he could go back in time and protect her.

But he'd never been any good at protecting anyone other than Angelica. This time, he vowed he would be. This time it was extremely important that he keep her safe. The tension that always rode him sharpened and he shivered under the pressure it presented. He should get up and leave. Now. Before this thing went any further and he lost the little bit of sense he had.

But he stayed all the same.

* * *

She'd suggested a movie and they'd watched *The Sixth Sense*. He knew he should have left earlier, but he'd been unable to make himself go.

"This is nice."

"Nice" again. He knew what she was doing. Creating a barrier between them so that she'd didn't feel too much. He knew that he had no business being here with this woman. He was going to hurt her no matter what he did. And hurting her wasn't something he could live with.

He wanted more from her. He didn't question why, only knew that he did. "It's getting late. Should I be heading home?"

She sat bolt upright and looked at him with those wide gray eyes. She was trying to shutter them as she usually did, but there was no real chance for her to do so. Good job, old man. Go right for the jugular every time.

"I'm sorry. I guess that wasn't subtle."

"No, it wasn't."

"If we're going to get to know each other…" He let the sentence trail off, unwilling to be even more of a hypocrite than he was. He wanted to know every intimate detail of her life to figure out what had shaped her into the woman she was today, but he'd never share those same things about himself with her.

"Rand, we work together."

"Unless I've lost my touch we're going to do more than work together."

"Well…"

"I'm not a heartless seducer," he said.

"I wouldn't mind if you were," she said.

"You lost me, sweetheart."

"I'm not looking for anything long-term here. My career is finally on track, and if I play my cards right I could be a VP in the next year or so."

"What does that have to do with me?" he asked, not sure he liked being set up as her stud.

"Everything. I can't afford to get involved with a man."

"What does that make me?" he asked. He definitely didn't like this setup.

"You're a man but you're also one of those guys who has a new girl with him every month."

"I see." It bothered him to realize that she had noticed his predilection. Maybe this was her way of protecting herself.

"Do you really understand?" she asked.

"No."

She took his hand in hers. "I...oh, God, this is harder than I thought it would be."

"Just spit it out."

"Well, I thought you weren't a long-term kind of guy."

"Usually I'm not." Rand had learned a long time ago that leading a charmed life extended only to the outer perception.

She wrinkled her nose, something he noticed she did when she wasn't sure of herself. It might be endearing if he wasn't listening to her say she wasn't as deeply affected by him as he was by her.

"At this point in my life I can't have more than an affair with you," she said in a rush.

He leaned back. *An affair.* The purely masculine part of him said so be it. He wanted her in his bed, and he didn't have to make any kind of emotional connection to her. But his soul—that wounded sixteen-year-old boy deep inside—warned it was too late. That not getting involved with his woman physically was the only way to escape unscathed.

He wasn't the kind of man who should be involved with someone who threatened his self-control. He was more comfortable in complete control. And Corrine had other needs. She needed the kind of man who could give her the family she'd never had growing up. The kind of man who didn't have problems of his own.

Rand put his arm around her and tugged her to him until she rested right next to him. He tilted her head back and took her mouth in a deep, searing kiss. He tried to tell himself it was an experiment to see if she could still say she was objective at the end of it. He tried to tell himself it was to prove a point to her. He tried to keep it purely physical, but he couldn't.

She moaned deep in her throat and her mouth opened for his, her tongue curling around his and making teasing forays into his mouth. Her hands clutched his shoulders, fingernails biting through the thin barrier of his shirt. She shifted on the couch until she was straddling his lap, and her hands left his shoulders to hold his face. Her mouth was as much a participant as his. In fact, if he'd let her, he knew she'd take control of the embrace.

He didn't let her. He'd learned long ago that surrendering any type of control wasn't a good idea. He slid his hands down her back, tugging down the zipper of her dress as he went. She wasn't wearing a bra under the sundress, and he contented himself with caressing her spine and the sides of her breasts for long minutes. Until she thrust her hips against his. Settling her mound right over his aching erection.

He took her buttocks in his hands and pressed her down against him. She felt so damned good. He held her to him and thrust slowly. She lifted her mouth from his and stared down at him, her eyes wide and questioning. He thrust against her again.

"It'll kill me to stop but I need to know that an affair is okay with you."

He thought about it. Knowing himself and his weaknesses, he should get up and leave. But he was rock hard and holding a lapful of woman who excited him more than any had before. And frankly, leaving wasn't an option. "At this point I'd agree to anything."

"I know," she said.

He took a deep breath. He didn't want to stop. He couldn't stop. And her attitude seemed to be the best one—for him. If she wanted a red-hot affair he could give her that. "Okay."

She smiled and shrugged her shoulders until the bodice of her dress fell around her waist. And then she leaned toward him. Her naked breasts pillowed on his chest, her mouth lowering toward his.

She kissed him the way he liked it, hot and deep. He focused solely on the physical. If all she wanted was this, he'd make it the best either of them had ever had. Rand Pearson didn't do things by half measure and he always played to win.

Though she was in the dominant position she knew she wasn't in charge. She hadn't been in charge of herself or anyone else since she'd gotten in the car with him earlier today. This entire episode marked a departure from the person she'd always believed herself to be. And she was glad to see this new woman emerging tonight.

Rand wasn't her kind of guy. She usually preferred men who were bland and ordinary. No, that wasn't right. Just being with him made the others seem bland.

Rand made her feel things too sharply for her to really be able to control them. She'd decided on an affair as the only safe way to burn out the fire that raged between them and to protect herself. Her mind said she'd made the wrong choice, but her body rejoiced in that decision.

She felt flooded with sensations that were generated by the man underneath her. Her center was dewy and wet, and though he wasn't touching her—only watching her—she felt like he was caressing her skin.

He palmed her breasts, plumping them up and staring at her closely. She'd always felt too small in the chest department, but the look in his eyes said he found her just right.

"You're so pretty here," he said, dropping soft kisses on the globes of her breasts.

A feeling of voluptuousness assailed her. She thrust her shoulders back, hoping to entice him closer. He murmured his approval. One of his hands burrowed through her hair and urged her to arch her back even farther.

"That's it, baby."

But he didn't move any closer to her aching flesh. Instead, he kept about an inch of space between his mouth and her nipple. Each exhalation of breath brushed over her, like a silk scarf. Bringing her aroused body to rigid attention.

She tried to move her hands to his head, to force his mouth onto her flesh, but he grasped both of her wrists in one of his big hands. She tried to shift to bring them closer together but he controlled her easily.

"Why?" she asked when it became apparent he wasn't going to move until he was ready.

He brought his mouth to her collarbone and whispered the words against her skin. She shivered. The sensation made her feel so acutely aware of herself as a woman. His woman.

"Because waiting makes the pleasure more exquisite," he said.

He was right, but she didn't want him to crash through any more barriers. They were just having sex.

It wasn't supposed to feel like this. "I can't take much more."

"Oh, yes you can."

He gave her a wicked grin. This time he scraped his teeth from the base of her neck down her chest, stopping at the globes of her breasts. He repeated the caress until every part of her body was on fire. She was unable to keep her hips from rolling against him.

"Rand," she moaned.

"Want more?" he asked, breathing right over her nipple this time. His mouth was so close, she felt the humidity of his words.

"I'll get even," she said, hardly recognizing the breathy voice as her own.

"Give me your breast," he said.

She shifted her shoulders, and this time he supported her back and finally she felt his lips close over her nipple. Again he waited. Not sucking on her but letting her hardened nipple fill his mouth. She needed more. The ache between her legs was growing stronger. Rocking against his erection no longer satisfied it, but intensified it. She wished they were both naked.

Needed them both to be naked. She tugged her wrists free of his grip. She unbuttoned his shirt and caressed the rock-hard planes of his chest. He began to suckle at her breast. His hands roamed over her back down to her waist, then slid underneath the barrier of her clothing to cup her buttocks again.

He bit lightly on her nipple and thrust his hips up

toward hers at the same time. The sensation was incredible. She shuddered and moaned his name.

"Like that?" he asked, moving to her other breast.

"*Like* is too tame a word."

He suckled her other nipple until she felt that she'd explode. He pulled back just short of that. "Rand, please."

"Not yet. Will you strip for me?"

She didn't know if she could do it. Her first instinct was to open his pants, free him and take him. But Rand had made her feel more during foreplay than most of the men she dated. And she wanted to please him.

"Okay."

She climbed off his lap and pushed her dress and panties off in one swift movement and then returned to him.

"That was the quickest striptease in history."

"You wanted a show?"

"Hell, yeah."

"I might be persuaded to do a little more for you, but you're going to have to lose your clothes."

"Happy to oblige."

He shrugged out of his shirt and then stood to remove his shorts and boxers with a quickness that belied his need to go slowly. There was a fine line of hair that tapered down his belly to his groin. He was...bigger than she'd expected him to be. He noticed her staring and held his hand out to her.

"Enough waiting?" he asked, with a gentleness she hadn't realized he had.

"Oh, yes."

He hugged her to him. And she nestled against his chest. Her blood pounded through her veins and the scent of him surrounded her. His heart beat a steady tattoo under her cheek. He settled back on the couch, pulling her over him and taking her mouth in one of those deep kisses of his that made her question why this had to only be temporary.

While his mouth consumed hers, his hands swept over her body. She settled over him. Felt his erection probing at her entrance. He pulled back.

"Are you on the pill?"

"Yes," she said. No way would she ever bring an unwanted child into the world.

"I'm clean. Gave blood last month," he said.

"Me, too," she said. In fact, she'd seen him at the blood drive.

"Ready?"

"Almost," she said.

His roaming hands found the aching flesh between her legs, seeking out the center of her desire and caressing her lightly. His other hand stayed at the small of her back, urging her hips to rock against him. She felt everything inside her start to tighten, and knew that the end was near. She wanted him inside her.

Reaching between their bodies, she took him in her hand and guided him to her entrance. He held her hips in both of his hands and lifted his mouth from hers.

"Ride me," he said.

She did. She felt too full at first and had to wait for her body to adjust to him. Then she started moving on him. Braced her hands on his shoulders and tilted her head back because the expression in those deep green eyes of his made her feel things too intensely.

She kept the pace steady until everything inside of her tightened and her climax washed over her. Rand's hands on her hips changed from guiding to controlling. He held her still for his thrusts. He suckled strongly on her breast and surged up into her three times before he came with a shout of release that echoed in her mind.

He hugged her to him, letting the sweat dry on their bodies. And Corrine could only think that Rand was never going to be a temporary man in her life. She would be remembering him and this moment until the day she died.

Six

"That was nice," Corrine said long minutes later.

"Nice, huh?"

"Oh, yeah. I never knew that I could share something so profound with a man."

Profound? He didn't do profound. In fact, she'd insisted it was just a red-hot affair. Why then had it felt like soul sex? The kind of physical bonding that he'd always dismissed as bragging by other men, and fantasy by the women they'd shared it with.

He'd isolated himself from the world a long time ago. He worked hard to give the impression that he was open and gregarious, but the truth was he felt safest by himself. Felt most comfortable when he was in his dark cave. Why then did he have the urge to drag Corrine back there with him?

There were maybe three moments in his life that he'd felt this intensely since he'd given up the bottle. The first had been when Roger had died. The second had been when he'd joined Angelica to create Corporate Spouses. And tonight with Corrine in his arms he felt it again.

Something deep inside him shuddered and he wasn't sure he was going to be able to stay here. He needed to get away from her. To get away from this place where he felt too vulnerable. And there was no escape. She was murmuring something soft against his chest and he didn't want to separate their bodies and leave.

But he had to. He lifted her from him and she smiled shyly at him. The tension, always his constant companion, tightened the back of his neck. He stood abruptly, tugging on his pants and zipping them.

Her smile faded and she grabbed a blanket from the back of one of the end chairs and wrapped it around herself. She looked incredibly small standing there, her thick blond hair hanging around her shoulders, her gray eyes not frozen for once but alive with questions and a lingering desire. Her mouth was still swollen from his kisses. And there was a flush on her skin from the climax she'd just had.

Leaving now was the last thing he wanted. His recently satiated body still craved more. He needed to make her his again and again until he'd made her his completely. Until all her secrets had been found.

Inside his head a war raged. He wanted to stay. Hell, his body screamed he had to stay. He longed to scoop her into his arms and carry her down the hall to her bed. Then he would take her in every way he'd ever taken a woman.

He felt the man he was expected to be colliding with the man he really was. He gritted his teeth and clenched his fists.

"Rand?" Something in her voice revealed the vulnerability he'd never expected her to experience.

He glanced up at her. Why did he always seem to hurt those he wanted to protect? How many times was he going to have to fail at this before he learned the lesson?

"Are you okay?" she asked.

No. He'd never been okay. He'd been running all his life, and for the first time had met someone who made him want to stop. But he couldn't—wouldn't— stop now and bring her into his world. She deserved better. In fact, she wanted a better man—from him. She only demanded sex from him.

"I'm fine."

"You seem—"

"I'm okay. Listen, I've got to go." He walked around her living room, grabbing his clothing, shoving his boxers, socks and tie into his pockets and shrugging into his shirt.

"You don't have to leave."

"Yes. I do."

She trailed behind him to the door, and he knew that this wasn't what she'd had in mind. His body urged him to stay, as well. Stay through the night and twist with her on her bed. But he knew himself well enough that he had to leave now.

"I'll call you," he said.

"Don't bother."

"You're the one who wanted an affair."

"I know. But I didn't want it to feel like a one-night stand."

He pivoted to face her. He could tell she was trying to put on her office face, cool and calm, but instead she was wary. Watching him as if he were a dangerous animal. Hell, he felt dangerous and out of control. God, he needed something to numb him to this feeling.

"This isn't a one-night stand."

"You're right. It feels more like a quickie."

"Don't push me, woman. I'm trying to do what you asked."

"When did I ask for you to make me feel as if I'd just discovered fire and then to walk away?"

He dropped his jacket and moved toward her, then caged her face in his hands and tilted her head back so that she was defenseless to him. Bending his head, he took her mouth in a ruthless kiss. He expected her to be passive or rebuff him, but instead her hands grabbed his head and she gave him back the same kiss.

Damn, she was his equal on too many levels. He pulled back. Her mouth was full, lips wet and glistening from his kiss. His erection throbbed against his inseam and he knew that he wasn't in for a comfortable night. But comfort had walked out the door the day he'd met Corrine Martin.

"Next time we'll take all night," he said.

"Maybe there won't be a next time."

"Dammit, Corrine."

"Yes, dammit, Rand. I didn't sign up to be your plaything."

"But you expected me to be yours?"

"I didn't hear you objecting," she said.

"Show me a man who'd object when he has a willing woman on his lap."

She flushed. He knew he'd gone too far, but he was feeling trapped and his instincts always said to come out fighting.

"Goodbye, Rand," she said.

He grabbed his stuff and walked out the door. He heard it close quietly behind him.

Corrine knew a brush-off when she got one. She hoped she'd come out the winner of her last confrontation with Rand, but she knew deep inside there had been no winner. Just two losers.

Which was why she'd never let herself become involved with men she had to work with. Sure, there had been that incredible heat between them, but now all she could do was regret it. And she hated regrets because they were a useless waste of energy.

She'd been unable to sleep after he left so she'd spent the night doing new projections for the coming quarter. She worked through the rest of the weekend, telling herself that it didn't matter that he hadn't called. She didn't want to talk to him again.

But inside she felt the same way she had when she'd been six and Mrs. Tanner had told her she'd been found in a trash can. And that *no one* wanted her. Even though she'd said she only wanted an affair, she'd expected—okay, hoped for—more from Rand.

That was in the past. Today was Monday and she was ready for a busy week, dressed to the nines in a severe black Donna Karan suit that she'd purchased when she'd first been promoted. She loved the suit. It made her feel invincible.

She walked into Tarron and wanted to groan inside. Rand was standing in the lobby chatting with one of the security guards. She walked straight past him, not even glancing in his direction. Keep breathing, she reminded herself as she waited for the elevator doors to close.

They started to shut and she let her guard start to drop, but then a large, masculine hand blocked them and Rand stepped inside. He hit the button for her floor and then the button to close the doors.

"Good morning, Corrine," he said.

She nodded at him. Not really wanting to start an inane conversation that would mask what she really wanted to say, which was something mean and sarcastic. But she wasn't going to let him see how deeply he'd wounded her.

"Not talking to me today?" he asked, moving closer to her in the elevator.

"That would be childish," she said.

Her gut told her to step away from him, but she refused to give even the appearance of backing down. So she stood her ground, even though now she could see that he didn't look as well put together as he usually did. His tie was knotted perfectly, his suit neat and clean, but there was something different about him today.

"And neither of us are children," he said, facing her.

"What do you want from me?" she asked. She knew it was abrupt, but she didn't really know how to play games with men. She knew how to keep them at bay with an icy glare or a few well-phrased barbs, but shoving a man back outside her inner wall after she'd let him in…that was one thing she'd never attempted before.

He sighed. "A few minutes of your time."

"Why?" she asked, realizing he looked different today because of his eyes. He seemed tired. No, more like exhausted. She linked her fingers together to keep from reaching out and soothing the tension she could read in his face.

"I don't like this awkwardness between us," he said. This was more than she'd anticipated. There was a genuineness to him that she hadn't expected.

"Me, neither. I mean, we have to continue working together on the training project. And Paul would notice if I never claimed my other two dates."

"I wasn't talking about our business relationship."

"That's the only one we have, Rand." An affair was all she'd wanted. But after making love with

Rand one time she'd realized an affair would never be enough. That she wanted more from him than she'd ever be comfortable asking him for. Because if she did ask him to stay she'd have to open all of her vulnerabilities to him. And she'd learned an important lesson the other night: Rand Pearson wasn't a man she wanted to know her weaknesses.

"I disagree."

She swallowed, unsure what to say to him. She was swamped with emotions that eroded her confidence and made her feel inadequate, and she was a grown woman for God's sake. She wasn't going to let him make her feel that.

"Please, Cori. Just give me a chance to explain."

"Why should I?"

"I haven't slept since I left your place. I can't close my eyes without seeing you."

Why did he have to say things like that? He made her believe that maybe her instincts had been correct when she'd decided to make love with him.

"I asked Adam to give me fifteen minutes alone with you this morning."

"Why?" she asked.

"I thought the office would be the best place for us to talk."

She nodded. It would be a safe place. Neither of them would ever do anything to jeopardize their professional images.

Silence descended and then the doors opened on her floor. Adam, her assistant, was sitting behind his desk. "Hello, Adam. Any schedule changes for today?"

"Just Mr. Pearson. I left you a voice mail with all your updates."

"Thank you, Adam."

"Will you be with Mr. Pearson all morning?" Adam asked.

"No. Just fifteen minutes."

"I might need longer. I don't like to rush," Rand said.

She remembered the fierce look in his eyes when he'd left on Saturday night. For her own sake, she needed to get him in and out of her office as quickly as possible. But if she treated him any differently than she normally did she'd subject herself to gossip. And she didn't want to let that happen.

"I don't want to keep you," she said.

"I won't let you," he said.

She stepped into her office. Rand followed her. He smelled good—better than a man who'd left her should smell. She knew better than to let things go further between them. But her heart sometimes didn't listen to her mind. And this was one of those times.

Rand had no real plan in mind when he'd followed Corrine into her office. He only knew things couldn't continue the way they had been. He'd spent last night in a dark place he hadn't visited since his brother Charles's death so long ago.

A sealed bottle of Cutty Sark had been his only companion there. He hadn't broken the seal even though his hands had sweated and he'd reached for the bottle too many times to count.

Something had to be resolved with Corrine. And it had to be done today. He wasn't sure how much longer he could battle his need for a drink and his need for Corrine. He needed some kind of semblance of normalcy in his life.

He glanced around her office. He'd been in here twice before and he'd never noticed how cold it was. Only seeing her home had given him a glimpse of the real woman behind her corporate suits. And now he realized how well she hid herself. He knew the price for doing just that, because for years he'd been doing the same thing.

"What did you want to discuss?" she asked, seating herself behind her desk.

Her hands were primly folded on the surface, and he realized she was treating him the same way she treated all the other men she interacted with. She tucked a strand of hair back into the bun at her nape and then straightened her blotter.

"I'm not going to let you do it," he said, walking around her desk and propping one hip against the side.

"Do what?" she asked, tilting her head to meet his gaze.

Though he was in the dominant position, he felt the way he always did around her, that she held the power. Maybe that was part of what drew him to her. He only knew that he'd been raised to win, and whatever it took, he'd find a way to manage Corrine Martin. "Relegate me back to the role of stranger."

She shrugged and looked away. "Don't be ridiculous. I'd never do that."

"And I wouldn't let you. We've been too much to each other."

"Too much?" she asked, her voice a husky whisper.

"Lovers," he said, brushing his finger down the side of her face. She had the softest damned skin he'd ever touched. Whenever she was near him he wanted—no, needed—to touch her. His fingers actually tingled with the urge to feel her.

Her pupils dilated and he knew she was remembering their one time together. It wasn't enough. Would a million times be enough to get his fill of her? Would becoming so familiar with her lithe body appease the hunger that ran deep in his veins? He doubted it.

Nothing short of her complete surrender would satisfy him. And he knew damn well that wasn't in either of their best interests.

He had to touch her. Grabbing the arms of her chair, he swung it toward him. Sliding his legs along the side of the chair, he caged her.

She looked up at him, awareness in her eyes. A flush of arousal faintly tinted her cheeks. No longer was he a man to be kept at a safe distance.

"I thought I knew what I wanted from you, Rand. But I was wrong."

"What do you want?" he asked, knowing on one level they both had the same objective.

"I'm not sure. I only know that I can't handle a repeat of the other night."

Honesty was important now because he was keeping other secrets he'd *never* share. "Me, neither."

"I'm not looking for happily ever after," she said quietly. "Frankly, I've seen enough of life to doubt it exists, but there is something about you that makes me want to believe it. And I know that's a dangerous thing."

"Why is that a dangerous thing?" he asked, because it was easier than facing the truth that her words struck a chord deep inside of him. They'd both been shaped by a hard life, although he knew she'd never guess that he'd suffered as she had, albeit in a different way.

But how hard was it really? He'd been given every luxury and sent to the finest schools. When had he turned into such a whiner?

"I don't know. I've forced myself not to form attachments, and you're a playboy, so it should be easier with you than with any other man."

"I'm not a playboy."

"Please. You've had more women than James Bond."

"Does that excite you?"

"I don't know. But the thought of all the experience you have…all the things you've done that I haven't…it makes me feel inadequate."

"You're not."

"Usually I'm confident of myself in any arena, but you're used to dealing with upper executives and I'm still middle management."

"Corrine, don't belittle yourself. None of the women you've seen me with hold a candle to you."

She bit her lip nervously. He knew she wanted to ask more questions, saw it in her eyes, but she didn't. "What I meant before was that I'm trying to keep you from being more than a temporary affair, but it's not working. Even when I was saying I wanted something temporary with you, my body was saying 'no way, girl—this isn't a temporary thing.'"

Taking her shoulders in both of his hands, he urged her to stand. Pulling her close to his body, he held her. "I wish I could make you promises."

"Why can't you?"

"Because you can't have everything."

Their eyes met and she took a deep breath before she said, "I don't want everything, Rand…just you."

Seven

Corrine wasn't sure when she'd decided to ask for what she wanted in her personal life. It had started when she'd watched Rand drive away on Saturday night. It had grown all day Sunday when she'd realized that hedging her bets hadn't protected her from feeling washed-up and used. It had solidified when he'd said he couldn't close his eyes without seeing her.

She knew that she meant more to him than the temporary easing of some sexual ache. He held her closely, carefully. Made her feel like she was the most precious woman in the world. And she'd always dreamed of feeling that way.

Snuggling closer in his arms, she realized this wasn't the first time he'd held her so. There was a part of Rand that was as unsure as she was in this situation. She felt it in the way he watched her when they were alone.

She slid her arms around his waist under his jacket. Even in the trappings of corporate America he stood out. His suit was by a top designer, his scent totally male and his body rock hard. He wasn't a man who found his way to the top and was content to stay there. He kept climbing up when most people would be content to stop and enjoy the fruits of their labor.

He ran his hands up and down her spine, and she wished she'd gone to his house yesterday so they could have made love. But she knew this moment couldn't have come any sooner. It took her a while to puzzle things out in her head, and she knew she needed some reassurance from Rand that he still wanted her.

That reassurance was nudging at her belly. She slid her hands down his back to his buttocks and he groaned deep in his throat. She loved the way he reacted to her touch. She glanced up at him and he smiled ruefully.

"I know I'm at work, but my body doesn't care."

"We could…" There was a need deep inside her to cement the tentative bond they'd formed. To make him realize how deeply he needed her. She wasn't sure that he could ever really want her in any way that wasn't sexual, but she wanted to probe into their new relationship and find something that proved she wasn't the only one involved.

He tipped her chin up, brushed a featherlight kiss

against her mouth and then all across her face. She leaned up and found his mouth with hers. Tilting her head, she kissed him with all the pent-up longing that flooded her body. His hands on her face changed, supporting her head for the demands he made of her. He thrust his tongue deep inside her mouth, seeking out her secrets. Tasting her so completely that her entire body was sensitized to him.

She reached for his tie, started to loosen it, then unfastened the button underneath. He took her wrists in one hand, bit her lower lip gently and lifted his head.

''We can't. I'd never be happy with the five minutes we have left here. And neither would you.''

''You're right,'' she said. She wanted to explore him, and she promised herself the next time she had this man naked she was going to find out all the places he liked to be touched.

''I know.''

''Smart-ass.''

He just grinned at her, and she couldn't help herself from smiling. He set her back in her chair and walked around her desk. She wished the desk and office made her feel more professional, but for once they didn't. Even her career goals paled while he sat in her office. All she wanted was him. That thought scared her, shook her to her core. Who was she if she wasn't an executive?

''I'd like to take you to dinner tonight,'' he said.

''Sure,'' she said, knowing that they should take the time to get to know each other. Maybe even slow things down. Yeah, right. Who was she kidding? She'd never be satisfied with anything less than a full-out naked affair with this man.

He took his PalmPilot from his pocket and consulted his schedule. "I'm working until eight. How does nine sound?"

She wasn't sure she could do what Rand did. He worked all day teaching classes in business manners and etiquette and then spent all night at various corporate functions. Being "on" that often wasn't something she'd ever be comfortable with. "Do you really want to go to a restaurant?"

"No, I want to see you."

"Why don't you come to my place and I'll fix us dinner?"

"I'm not sure I'll be able to eat," he said.

"I'll make something that can be reheated."

"I'll bring dessert."

"I was thinking you were dessert," she said with a grin.

He straightened his tie and then stood, walking toward the door.

"Rand?"

"Yes?"

"Why did you leave the other night?"

He walked back toward her. "I'm used to being in control."

"So?"

"You make my control disappear, and that's not a comfortable place to be," he said.

"You do the same to me."

"I'm not like other guys, Cori."

"I don't think you're all that different," she said.

"You're right. Maybe it's ego or wishful thinking."

"I don't think it's ego," she said.

"Why not?"

"There's something solid about you, Rand."

He waggled his eyebrows at her and she knew he was trying to tease her into leaving off this conversation. "I hoped you'd notice."

She let him change the subject but promised herself she'd dig deeper later. "It's hard not to."

"Come over her and kiss me before I leave."

"Why?"

"Because it'll make the day shorter." She was helpless to deny him. And after she'd kissed him and he walked away, she worried that she was losing herself. Not so much because her goals no longer seemed important, but because for the first time it didn't matter if they weren't.

Rand was late. Traffic on I-4 was a bitch and unless he missed his guess it was going to be more like eleven when he got to Corrine's place. He'd had Kelly, his secretary, call Corrine and tell her he wasn't going to be able to make it. So why was he still heading for Kaley Street and her house?

He knew the answer. Despite the fact that he'd never been good at interpersonal relationships, there was a part of him that liked being near her. Even if he could just hold her and listen to her breathing he'd be content.

Twenty minutes later he parallel parked in front of her house and sat there. The same tension that always rode him was there, but being closer to Corrine tamed it—most of the time. Her lights were off and he knew he should just go home. But instead he grabbed his cell phone and dialed her number.

She answered on the first ring. Her voice was softer than it was in the office and he wondered what she was wearing. He'd noticed she changed her attitude with her clothing. "It's Rand."

"Hey," she said. Her voice was dreamy and sleepy. And he knew he should just put the car in Drive and go home.

"Did I wake you?" he asked. If he had, he'd leave. It'd kill him to go home to his dark, empty house in Winter Park, but he'd do it, dammit. He wasn't a cad. He was a Pearson. A gentleman through and through. No matter how high the cost, no one had ever seen him behave as anything but a gentleman. Corrine wasn't going to be the first.

"No. I'm reading. Long day?" she asked. He heard the springs of her bed creak as she changed positions. Or maybe it was only his imagination. He doubted it. He knew she was in bed…imagined her there wearing something slim-fitting and sexy.

"The longest." Made longer by the ache in his soul to claim this woman again. To make love to her until exhaustion took them both and he could no longer think.

"I'm sorry. I missed you at dinner."

Her words were a salve for his soul, for that weary part of himself that had been alone too long. She called to a part of his soul he'd walled off long ago and made him wish he was a better man. "Good."

She chuckled. "That's one of the things I like about you."

"What?" he asked.

"That self-confidence. I wish I had an eighth of it."

Would she still like him if she realized it was all a role he'd written for himself to play? He wasn't sure she would. He'd long ago decided he liked himself better when he was pretending to be the good son.

"Speaking of self-confidence…" Despite his training in manners and deportment he knew there wasn't a right way to invite yourself for a sleepover.

"Yes."

"Would you let me in if I showed up on your front door?" he asked.

"Maybe."

Damn, she kept him on his toes. "What would it take to make it a yes?"

He heard her sigh, then the sound of the bedsprings creaking again. If she turned him away he knew he was going to spend the night with the most lurid fantasies of her twisting beneath him on a creaking bed, with only the sounds of her moans and the bed filling the room.

"You did promise me dessert."

"I did, didn't I?" There had been no time to stop

at a bakery. But he had something for her that was just as satisfying as a chocolate dessert but with none of the calories.

"Mmm, hmm," Corrine said.

She was teasing him. He liked it. He thought this might be the problem with Corrine. He plain liked too much about her and he knew from experience and life that things he wanted the most were the ones he never got to keep. "You won't be disappointed. I guarantee it."

"Is that an ironclad, money-back guarantee?" she asked, her voice dropping a notch.

"Oh, yeah." He was getting hard, sitting in front of her house and talking to her. He wanted to be in there with her, to let her tease him while they were cuddled close to each other. So he could let things develop to their natural conclusion and then he'd make her forget all about teasing him.

"Where are you?" she asked.

"Parked outside your house."

"What if my answer is no?"

"Then I'll drive home and take a cold shower."

"Really?"

"Really," he said.

"I don't want to be responsible for that. Why don't you come in?"

He switched off the phone and tossed it on the seat. He didn't want to appear too eager, but hell, he'd just invited himself over. She had all the power in this situation. He didn't ring the bell since she knew he was out there.

She didn't turn on the lights, just opened the front door and stepped back. There was a faint light at the end of the hallway and he could barely make out her face. She wore a voluminous gown that flowed around her when she turned and walked back up the hall. Though not the slim-fitting one of his imagination—still sexy as hell. He closed and locked the door. And then followed her.

Her bedroom was large and had a sitting area off to one side. At first all he could do was stare at her bed. It wasn't overly large but had a wrought-iron bedstead that he immediately pictured her wrists tied to.

He should have guessed with all that creaking earlier that she'd have a bed made for sex. There was a mound of pillows at the head and he could still see the faint indentation from her body.

He glanced around the room. She'd set up a cold supper on the coffee table in the sitting area. He realized she'd been waiting up for him.

"What if I hadn't come by?" he asked, unsure of himself suddenly.

"I'd have been disappointed."

He was humbled.

"Come and eat. Then we can talk."

He knew he shouldn't let himself be so comfortable with her, but for once he silenced the voice inside his head. Shrugging out of his jacket, he sat on the love seat. Corrine curled up next to him as he ate. The tension that was always his companion grew a little tighter deep inside.

* * *

Despite the long day he'd put in, a kind of kinetic energy buzzed around Rand. He talked a little about his job and ate in a way that only a man could. She'd thought she'd kept out too much food, but he finished it all in rather little time.

A nervous excitement bubbled inside her. Rand made her feel alive in a dangerous and exciting way. A part of it was the way he watched her and made her aware of him as a man. The other part was…well… purely sexual.

She'd made her plans for the night very carefully. There were things she'd always wanted to try but she'd never trusted a man enough before. But things were different with Rand and with her. After watching him leave the last time, after being so totally at his mercy, she'd decided she'd be a full participant or none at all.

When he was done he turned to her with that white-hot gleam in his eyes. "Well?"

"Has your hunger been satisfied?" she asked. Having made her decision to see this thing between them through to the end, she felt free. It was as if she'd cast aside whatever inhibitions she had. She was going to enjoy every second of her time with Rand.

"One of them."

She stood, removing her white silk robe. His breath hissed in through his teeth and his eyes narrowed as he saw the white teddy and thigh-high hose she wore underneath. She'd never owned a piece of fancy lingerie before. Her drawers were stuffed with cotton bras and panties that were utilitarian. "Let's see what we can do about the other one."

Taking him by the hand, she led him to her bed. With a slight shove she forced him to sit on the edge of the mattress. "Take off your shoes and socks."

"Are you in charge tonight?" he asked.

"I did just feed you."

"You have a point."

He bent and removed his socks and shoes, then removed his belt and tie, as well. "That's enough."

He raised one eyebrow at her in that manner of his that now just excited her rather than annoyed her. "I'm all yours."

"Lean back on the bed."

He did. She knew it was now or never. Be gutsy. Starting at his neck she undid the buttons of his shirt and pushed it from his shoulders. When the shirt was at his elbows, she stopped pushing it off and tied the sleeves together very neatly. Trapping his arms.

He raised one eyebrow at her in question.

"You mentioned bondage," she said.

"I didn't imagine I'd be the one tied up."

"I did," she said with a grin.

"Go for it," he said.

"I intend to."

His chest had enticed her since she'd seen him bare it on the beach. And the last time they'd had sex she'd been too caught up in her own feelings to really learn what he liked. Tonight was her chance.

She scraped her nail lightly over his pectorals. The muscle jumped under her finger. She leaned down and blew gently on his nipple. It tightened and the surrounding flesh was covered with goose bumps. "Like that?"

"Hell, yes."

She lowered her head. Bracing her hands on his shoulders, she dropped butterfly kisses all over his chest. He tensed his arms, straining against his shirt as she neared his nipple. First she licked the flat brown flesh and then when he moaned, she bit very lightly. His hips lifted from the bed and he groaned deep in his throat.

The sound sent shock waves through her. She felt her own body growing heavy as she touched him. She trailed her mouth down his skin, licking and biting at his rock-hard abs and stomach. When she reached the barrier of his waistband, she settled back on her haunches and toyed with the button.

"Don't tease me."

"I thought you liked anticipation."

"Sweetheart, I'm going to explode in another minute."

"Good."

She bent and took the tab between her teeth, pulling it slowly down. Then she slid her hand inside the placket and fondled him through his underwear. His breath hissed through his teeth and his hands were fisted.

She knew he was reaching the breaking point. So was she. The flesh between her legs was moist and ready to be filled by him. She tugged his pants down, stopping again before they were completely off, leaving the fabric just below his knees.

She caressed the corded tendons in his thighs. Damn, he had nice muscles. And then traced the line of hair from his chest to his groin. His penis was hard and red. She tiptoed her fingers around him. Watched as he grew even larger at her touch. Bending, she dropped kisses on his thighs and the bottom of his abdomen, letting her hair brush over his erection.

"Now," he said.

Until that moment she hadn't realized that position had nothing to do with power. Just hearing his voice was enough to make her want to respond. But it was her show. She unfastened the snaps between her legs that held the teddy closed and then slid up over him.

The first touch of their naked loins made each of them sigh. She reached between their bodies and positioned him before sinking down on him.

She heard the fabric of his shirt rip a second before his hands came up. Fondling her breasts through the lace of her teddy. One hand snaked around her back and nudged her shoulders forward until her breasts dangled within reach of his hungry mouth. He suckled her and his hands caressed her legs and buttocks.

She gripped his shoulders as exquisite sensation flooded her. She was so close to the edge. She tipped her head back and tightened herself around his flesh and felt the first contraction sweep through her. He felt it, too, as he grabbed her hips and pulled her down into his thrusts. She moaned his name as her climax rushed through her. He released her nipple and thrust into her three more times before roaring his completion.

She sank down onto him and closed her eyes. Reality said this couldn't last, but she couldn't regret the time they spent together. She knew he'd leave her one day, but didn't dwell on that. Instead, she held him tightly in her arms and enjoyed his strength and warmth.

Eight

Rand kicked off his pants and threw aside the remains of his shirt. She watched him warily, as if not sure how he'd react to her bondage play. And he wanted to keep her guessing.

If only for a few more minutes. The woman was too sexy for her own good. Fulfilling fantasies he'd only admitted to having to himself.

She held all the cards in this thing between them. She'd surprised him this evening. He'd have expected her, the women he'd come to know after a year of working together, to have refused to let him come into her home. But this was a new Corrine.

The soft Corrine, with her hair down and her sexy lingerie, touched the tender part of his soul. The part that had stopped growing the night Charles had died in the car.

The need for her was so all-consuming that it washed away his longing for the bottle. At least temporarily. He pushed those thoughts away and concentrated on the lovely blonde who was all his.

"Your turn," he said. He was having an X-rated fantasy involving her hose binding her wrists to the wrought-iron headboard. He wanted to hear the springs on the bed creak as he thrust into her hips. He wanted to love her slowly and for a long time.

One time wasn't enough. Hell, twice wasn't enough. There was a part of him that feared he'd never get his fill of her. And he already had one thirst that could never be quenched, he didn't need another one.

"What did you have in mind?" she asked.

He knew she meant the words to sound flirty but they came out worried. "You should have thought of the consequences of your actions. You know I play to win."

She scooted back on the bed, reaching around for her robe. That white silk that made her look untouchable.

"You liked it, don't deny it," she said.

"I loved every second of it. But that doesn't mean I don't want my chance to be in charge."

"You're always in charge. I'm not sure I can surrender my control."

"I did it."

"Your will kept you my captive. You broke the bonds easily."

"Do you honestly believe I'd do anything to hurt you?"

"No," she said, the word barely a whisper.

He expected more of the teasing play that they'd fallen into. But instead her eyes were very serious and he knew he'd stumbled into one of the secrets she was keeping. It was funny how they both had things they didn't want to discuss. Was this a healthy relationship? He doubted it. But then he'd never really had a healthy one.

He crawled up next to her. Propped two pillows against the headboard and then tugged her down until she was in his arms, her head resting right over his heart. She made him feel bigger and stronger than he was. For her he'd fight battles. For her he wanted to be better than he was and that scared him.

"What are you afraid of?" he asked.

She swallowed and looked away. "I don't want to talk about that."

"Tell me," he said, tipping her head back so their gazes met.

She walked her fingers over his chest. He sensed her intent was not to arouse him but to distract him, yet his body couldn't tell the difference and he felt himself start to harden. It was too soon, he thought. He shouldn't want her again—not yet.

"Promise not to laugh."

"Promise," he said. What had he done to convince her that he'd ridicule whatever she'd reveal to him?

He knew then that he couldn't just want to be better than he'd been before. He *had* to be better. Or he'd wind up hurting Corrine in ways he didn't want to.

"I'm not sure where you fit in my world."

"I think I fit nicely right here," he said, tightening his arms around her.

"I don't have a personal life. Just work, and the lines don't blur...or they haven't until you."

"Corrine, I'm not getting it."

"You know I was an orphan. Well, I created a picture-perfect image in my head of what my home life should be. I've created that here. It's a nice, safe world that I don't have to worry about losing."

"What does this have to do with me?"

"You don't fit here."

Her words cut him and he couldn't help it; he stiffened and pulled away.

But she cupped his jaw and gave him the most exquisite kiss. It was deep and carnal but at the same time touched something emotional inside that he was uncomfortable admitting he felt.

"I never put another person in this equation and I'm flying blind here."

"I'd say you did pretty well tonight."

"Well, I've always wanted to try some different things but never trusted a man enough to do it."

He rubbed her arm and felt that tension deep inside him squeeze tighter. "I don't know that I fit in your world here. But I think I could provide you with a place to experiment."

"I'm not just talking about sex."

"Of course you aren't."

"I mean sex is a part of it, too, but not just the only thing I want from you."

"What else do you want to do? Find your parents?" he asked, wanting to understand.

"No."

"Why not? It might give you some closure." Closure was something that had given him some peace. He still had to visit Charles's grave on the anniversary of his death. He still had to celebrate his brother on their birthday. Closure for him had come with remembering that just because a person died didn't mean they'd never lived.

"They threw me in a trash can, Rand. They wanted nothing to do with me."

A shiver walked across his spine, and he held Corrine tighter until he had a leash on his rage against the people who'd tossed her aside with little thought for how that would affect the child they'd brought into the world.

Then he made slow, sweet love to her, removing every stitch of her clothing first. Then kissing her from head to heels and back again. Her hands alternately returned his caresses and clutched at him as if she was afraid he'd leave her. He cherished every inch of her with his mouth, and when they both couldn't stand another minute of separation, he slid into her body.

Only when he was buried deep inside her body and she was moaning her climax did he let loose the feelings pouring through him. Finding his own satisfaction with this woman who was too vulnerable for a man whose greatest accomplishment was that he hadn't had a drink in almost ten years since he and Angelica had started working together.

He didn't think that would be enough. Because he knew that Corrine needed more and he also was sure she'd never ask for anything more from him. Someone who'd been left time and again was used to being disappointed. And he had only just realized that he'd rather die than disappoint her.

Corrine woke up in the middle of the night with a feeling that all was right in her world. It scared her. She'd spent so much time protecting herself that Rand had slipped under her guard. Not unnoticed, of course, but his presence was shocking all the same.

It was funny, really, but she liked having him there. For so long she'd been lonely on a very intimate level. She'd had lovers before, but they'd never made her feel anything near as transcendental as Rand had made her feel. Even the memories of what they'd shared were more shattering than actual consummation with other men.

Lying on her side, she felt Rand curled against her back. He held her with a fierce tenderness that made her hope she affected him as deeply as he affected her. She was surrounded by him. And in the middle of the night with no one around to witness it, she wrapped her fingers around his wrist, snuggling back against him. She felt safe.

It was a new feeling and one that frightened her.

Rand would leave, she knew this and she would mourn that loss. Because for the first time since she was six years old she really felt as if she'd found the seeds of a home.

Even just a temporary home would be fine with her. She knew he wouldn't stay forever. From what she'd observed, few people did last longer than five to ten years together. She'd take whatever time she was given with Rand because tonight was the first time she felt as if another person really cared about her.

When she'd tied his arms and had her wicked way with him, she realized that fun was an important part of relationships and she'd never relaxed enough in the past to actually enjoy anything close to what she'd found with Rand.

Finally she understood her power as a woman. It wasn't to dominate men, though it had been heady to have Rand under her and at her mercy. It was something different. Maybe just the knowledge that she had some power. That she didn't have to wait for life to happen to her. She could go out and make it happen.

Rand moved restlessly behind her and she turned to face him. Touching his face gently, she felt the wild pumping of his pulse. He kicked the covers off the bed and he jerked and groaned. Then a scream was ripped from his throat.

"Wake up, Rand," she said, leaning over him and stroking her hands down his torso. "You're here with me. Everything's okay," she said, repeating the words until his eyes opened.

Sweat covered his body and tension gripped his wiry frame. He sat up and rubbed his eyes with the heels of his hands. She was powerless to do anything to help him.

What did he dream about? Why hadn't she realized he had his own demons? That a man who wanted something temporary wasn't sometimes just looking for sex. Sometimes he was running from circumstances just as powerful as the ones that had shaped her.

"Are you okay?" she asked. Even to her ears the question sounded inane, but she didn't know what else to say. She was dealing with too many things right now. Her own feelings of need and now her knowledge that she'd overlooked a very important part of this man who'd become so significant to her.

He pushed her hands away. "Yeah, fine. Sorry about that."

She laced her fingers together and stared at the pillow, not his face. He was awake, but the feelings engendered by his dream still seemed to be with him.

"No problem. Do you want to talk about it?" she asked.

"No."

"Sure?" Why couldn't she just let it be? She didn't know, but she hated seeing him this way. She wanted to pull him into her arms and comfort him. To soothe his troubles and promise him that everything would be okay, even though she knew such promises to be false. Rand made her want to vow she'd do everything in her power to protect him.

"Corrine," he said. Just her name. A warning, she guessed, to back off.

She needed to do something. Her arms felt empty from not holding him the way he'd held her earlier when she'd confessed her dark, ugly secret. But she knew he wouldn't welcome that embrace.

"Want me to get you some water?" she asked.

He nodded. "I'll be fine in a minute."

She slipped her robe on and went into the bathroom, and returned, bringing him back the drink. He'd put his pants on in the short time it had taken her to get the water. She wondered if his dream had left him feeling vulnerable.

Of course it had. She'd felt the same way when she'd brought him into her room and let him see she'd been waiting for him. "Here you go."

"Thanks," he said, stalking to the window and staring out at the world covered in shadows. He tipped his head back and drained the glass in one long swallow.

"I don't think I'm going to be able to sleep anymore tonight."

She thought talking about whatever had woken him would be best, but it was clear he didn't want to. She wasn't sure what else to do until her eyes lit upon the thigh-high hose she'd had on earlier. She didn't want him to leave. Didn't want him to be alone now and didn't want to be alone herself.

"Come back to bed, Rand," she said, holding out her hand.

"You need to sleep. I shouldn't have come here tonight."

"Yes, you should have. I don't pretend to know what's going on between us, but we need each other. Now, come over here."

He still hesitated.

"I need you," she said.

Still he didn't move.

"Earlier I let you calm me."

"That was different."

"Why, because I'm a woman?"

He shrugged. She knew she'd struck close to the truth. She just waited.

"I don't want comfort from you, Corrine."

"What do you want?"

"Solace."

She understood. She let her robe drop from her body and opened her arms to him. He took two steps toward her and stopped.

"That's not fair to you."

"Let me decide what's fair."

He closed the gap between them and picked her up, settling her in the middle of the bed. There was no slow-building seduction this time. Rand suckled her breast and his hands went straight to her sweet spots, arousing her to the flash point quickly.

He made her feel everything too intensely, but she was aware for the first time that there was a part of himself he was keeping in check. She tugged his face down to hers and kissed him, but he pulled back. And when their eyes met she saw the struggle inside him.

He rolled her over onto her stomach, kissed the length of her spine and then took the pillows from the head of the bed and piled them beneath her hips. He slid into her from behind, his hands gripping hers and his body covering hers completely. His breath rasped in her ear, hot and desperate, as he drove them both toward the pinnacle.

She came once and felt him still hard inside her. He pulled out of her body and turned her over, tossing the pillows on the floor. Then lowered his head once more to her breast. He entered her again and moved with slow thrusts until she started to rise to meet him again. Then he increased the pace until they both climaxed with shattering intensity.

She closed her eyes and curled her arms around him. She held him tightly to her, never wanting to let him go.

Rand liked his office and enjoyed the fact that Corporate Spouses was the one place where he felt totally in control. Angelica was predictable, even though she'd started to get a little more emotional with her pregnancy hormones. Still, he knew how to handle her. Kelly, their secretary, could be counted on to be irreverent and sassy.

"Hey, boss man, Corrine is on line one for you," Kelly said through the open office door. Despite being only twenty-two, the secretary kept the office running smoothly and the mood light, even when they were having a crazy day.

Rand reached for the handset. It had been two

weeks since that night in Corrine's bed when he'd awakened from a nightmare of twisted metal and bloody regrets.

Frankly, he wasn't sure what to say to her. But she'd called at the office and this was one time he couldn't dodge her call as he'd been doing.

"Hello, Corrine."

"I know this is short notice, but I need to use our second date from the package I bought—tonight," she said, all business.

"The timing is bad." He had three classes this afternoon and he'd just fired one of only three of the men Corporate Spouses employed. There were more and more women executives who needed escorts to functions.

"I'm sorry for the short notice. Paul just gave me the Cortell account and mentioned the dinner. I could go alone, but this is really important to my career."

"I know how important your career is."

"So is yours," she said.

"What time?" he asked. He wasn't going to let her go alone. Even if he wasn't sure of his own control, he knew that he still couldn't willingly disappoint her.

"Eight at the Samba Room. It's over near Metro West."

"I've been there before. Want me to pick you up?" he asked.

He liked the Latin-flavored restaurant. He knew that Corrine would, too. It was just the kind of place that he should have invited her to. Would have invited her to on some semblance of a normal date if she hadn't seen him sweating in the middle of the night.

But she had, and it didn't matter that *he* knew where *she* was most vulnerable. He had to deal with her knowing his weakness, though he didn't want anyone to know he wasn't invincible. Especially not Corrine.

"Pick me up at my house. Angelica's been to dinner with the Cortells before so she can brief you on them. Jeff Cortell just sold us his yacht-building company. I e-mailed the information I have on it to Kelly."

"We're set, then," he said.

"I guess so."

Silence buzzed on the line. He wanted to say something but felt inadequate to the task. He didn't know what to say to reassure her and still protect himself. He hadn't slept any better by himself than he had in her bed that night two long weeks ago.

"You still there?" she said.

"Yes," he said curtly. He clicked on his e-mail icon and opened up his in-box. He needed a distraction. She wanted to talk about their relationship and he still wasn't sure what had happened the other night. Was it Corrine who'd brought back the dream? He hadn't had that one in almost ten years.

"I..."

He waited. He should make it easier for her. That's what a gentleman would do. But hell, he knew the truth. Underneath his breeding he was a real beast. So he let her stammer her way through the conversation even though he wanted to put her at ease. Anything to keep himself safe.

"I've missed you."

God, he'd missed her, too. His body craved her more than it ever had alcohol. He'd caught glimpses of her at Tarron when he'd been in the building to teach his training class. But he'd avoided her. She was a new weakness, and the only way he'd ever managed his weaknesses was to avoid them altogether.

"I guess I shouldn't have said that."

"I'm not good with this kind of thing," he said at last. Her voice was usually cool and well modulated, but when she spoke to him he heard the nuances of her emotions. And it only happened when they were alone.

She'd kept so much of herself locked away he felt as if he'd been chosen for the grand prize that she'd selected him to let her guard down with. Yet at the same time he didn't want the prize. The price he had to pay was too damned high.

"What kind of thing?" she asked.

What could he say? He knew men were supposed to be enlightened and more in touch with their emotions these days, but the plain truth was he felt better when he was just reacting. "Talking about how I feel."

"I'm not asking you to talk," she said.

But she was. He didn't call her on it. More silence on the line and then she sighed.

"I'll see you later."

"Corrine?

"Me, too," he said.

She sighed. "Was admitting you missed me so hard?"

"Yes."

"Then I'll have to reward you."

"That sounds interesting."

"You did say I could experiment with you."

"Yes, I did."

"Somehow I thought we'd be spending more time together," she said.

He wanted her. Each night he went home and fought between his twin desires—that damned un-opened bottle of Cutty Sark and his physical need for this woman who made him feel like the soft under-belly of a turtle. The rest of the world didn't realize he had that vulnerability.

He hadn't been sleeping well because when he closed his eyes he was plagued with dreams of her soft, sexy body, welcoming his. And he knew she wouldn't turn him away if he showed up at her door in the middle of the night. But he couldn't use her that way. Wouldn't add more pain to a life that had already been filled with it.

"Work has been crazy," he said.

"I know," she said.

"Hell, that's an excuse."

She said nothing. He wished he were in the same room with her so he could see her. So he could touch her and put an end to this conversation he didn't want to have.

"I wouldn't hurt you for anything," she said quietly.

"I'm used to being the strong one," he confessed.

"Oh, Rand. You still are the strong one. Sometimes you need someone to stand beside you."

She hung up the phone and he realized the truth of her words. But standing shoulder to shoulder meant being equal to the task, and he never knew when his own demons would spring out and render him incapable.

Nine

Corrine was nervous. And she didn't like it. She'd worked hard to get respect from her boss and here she was about to blow it. It was ten till seven. Rand should be at her place any minute, and instead of running stats in her head about the Cortell yacht company, she was debating if she should wear her silver or gold jewelry with the Ann Taylor pantsuit she'd purchased on her way home from work.

And it wasn't Jeff Cortell she was worried about impressing. Biting back a scream of frustration, she shoved her silver hoops in her ears and left the bedroom. She wasn't getting changed again. Snap out of it, girl. It's time to be an executive, not a woman.

Her perfect world was changing and she wasn't sure she liked it. She knew there was little she could do to stop the change. Well, there was one thing she could do, but not seeing Rand wasn't something she was willing to do. She liked him. She wanted him in her bed and in her life for as long as fate would let them be together.

She'd missed him the last few weeks they'd been apart. Especially late at night.

The doorbell rang and she collected her purse. She checked her appearance again in the mirror. Damn, did she have time to go back and get the gold earrings? Instead, she opened the door.

Rand looked like a cover model for *GQ* as usual. His tie was the same striking green as his eyes and perfectly knotted. He looked as if he'd effortlessly put himself together. She'd bet he hadn't stood in front of the mirror debating his appearance. She envied him that self-confidence.

"Hello. Traffic is heavy tonight so we'd better go."

"I'm ready. Did you get a chance to read the info I sent over on Cortell?"

"Before we talk business…"

"Yes."

He put his hands on her face and kissed her deeply and thoroughly. She was breathing heavily when he pulled away. He hadn't touched her hair or her clothing so she knew she was still presentable, but inside she felt rumpled and wished they didn't have to be anywhere.

"Nice outfit," he said, taking her key from her hand and locking the front door.

"You think so? What about the earrings?" she asked before she could stop herself. What was she, sixteen?

But she hadn't dated when she was sixteen. In fact, the men she'd had relationships with in the past had been more like ships passing in the night. One of the men had been an E.R. doctor who'd worked weird hours. The other one a traveling salesman who was only in Orlando two days each month.

This was a new type of relationship for her, she told herself. It was okay to be insecure. Except that Rand didn't make her insecure—he made her want to be more womanly than she'd been before. And she'd never been sure of what that entailed.

"Your earrings are fine."

"Just fine?" she asked. What the hell was wrong with her? She was about to have a panic attack over clothes. She couldn't believe this.

It was more than wanting to be Rand's equal. She knew that. It was more than wanting to impress Jeff Cortell for Paul, who was counting on her. Her job didn't hang in the balance of this one dinner. It was...oh, damn, she thought it might be that her world was changing and she wasn't ready for it.

"Nice?" Rand waggled his eyebrows at her. She knew he was teasing.

"Nice?"

"Cori, what's up with you?" he asked.

I'm having a mental breakdown because I've only just realized that you mean more to me than my job. And no person had ever meant that much to her.

That's not true—her birth parents had meant that much until she'd turned six and had her illusions shattered.

It wasn't the earrings, she realized. It was her. She'd never felt like this before. Rand stared at her as if she were going to freak out at any second. *Pull it together.* "Nothing. I knew I should have worn the gold earrings."

He led her to the car, then went around to climb in, but when he sat down he didn't start the engine. He turned to face her, one arm resting on the back of her seat.

"We're not leaving until you tell me what's wrong," he said.

The sincerity in his tone touched her. He cared about her, but then she'd already guessed that. There was something different about Rand when they were together. And maybe that was the thing that scared her so deeply.

"I don't know. I've never had any problem picking out clothing, but tonight I changed three times. I'm sure I'm wearing the wrong earrings, and for the first time *ever* I'm not thinking about my career."

"Sweetheart, you are gorgeous in whatever you wear, and earrings on your ears only enhance that image." He rubbed her neck while he spoke.

She knew he meant the touch to be soothing, but instead he was starting a fire throughout her body. It had been too long since they'd touched. Too long since he'd lifted one eyebrow at her in that lord-of-the-manor way of his. Too long since she'd touched him.

"Is that a line?" she asked.

"Is it working?"

She laughed and nodded. "Thanks."

"Nervous about the Cortells?" he asked.

"This is my first big account. I don't want to blow it."

"You won't."

"I wish I had your confidence."

"You do," he said.

He started the car and drove them to the Samba Room. The entire way she let his faith in her flow over her. It was heady to know that for once she had someone else on her side.

The Cortells were as affable as Angelica had said they were. Despite Corrine's worries in the car, she was effervescent, easily charming both Jeff and Alice. Corrine knew her job, and as Rand watched her interact with her clients he had a glimpse of what the future could hold for her. Tarron wasn't like other Fortune 500 companies in which women faced a glass ceiling. Paul Sterling was well aware of what the opposite sex could do and would promote on merit regardless of sex.

Rand was a little awed to realize that Corrine would probably be a VP in six months when Ross Chambers retired. Corrine had worked hard for her success, and he realized as he watched her work the table that she deserved a man who could share that with her. A man who brought to the relationship the skills needed to be successful in life.

Could he be that man?

They'd ordered wine with dinner. An expensive label from California and the smell of the alcohol had overwhelmed him. The lure of it was almost too much temptation. He had a glass sitting in front of him. He drained his water glass about five times but still he was thirsty.

The tension that had been getting stronger these past weeks without Corrine tightened even more and he felt that he wasn't going to escape it. He reached for his wine glass. Just one sip and he'd be okay. One sip and he'd— Hell. He stood abruptly. He needed a hell of a lot more than one damned sip of some wimpy wine.

"Rand?"

"Please excuse me," he said. With all the damned water he drank, let them think he was going to the bathroom.

He stalked out of the restaurant and found company with the smokers. Ha, his fellow addicts condemned by society to hang out in the front of establishments and puff away.

A guy in an Armani suit offered him a smoke but Rand declined. Smoking had never been his vice.

"My wife thinks cigarettes are gauche. Yours?" he asked.

"I'm not married."

"Even though I've been relegated outside I don't regret marrying her."

Paul Sterling had shared a similar sentiment with Rand. Seemed happily married men didn't mind making sacrifices for the women they loved. Rand didn't expect to ever be in their crowd. Being happily married would require him to talk about the things he held most private, and he couldn't imagine having that conversation with any woman, especially Corrine.

The Armani-suit guy left. Rand stared out at the parking lot and the busy cars on Sand Lake Road. He usually handled the presence of liquor better than he was doing tonight. For some reason his defenses were down and he thought he understood why. Corrine.

"Rand?"

He glanced over his shoulder to see Corrine standing there. She looked like salvation, with the restaurant lights shining behind her. Illuminating her as if she'd come from heaven to rescue him. But he'd found out long ago that no one was coming to rescue him. He would have to be the one to rescue himself.

"Yeah?" he asked. One time he'd like to be able to face his demon and feel as if he'd come out the winner. One time he'd like to be able to feel like the strong man he knew everyone expected him to be. One time he wanted…hell he wanted to feel normal.

"You okay?" she asked.

He nodded. Somehow saying no would make him feel like a wimp. "Just needed a breath of fresh air."

She crossed to him, standing so close he could smell her perfume. Damn, if she wasn't the sexiest woman he'd ever met. She was still in business mode, so it wasn't as if she were trying to seduce him, yet he was seduced. Her scent, her looks, her touch on his wrist. Soft and warm, reminding him that for tonight at least he wasn't alone. "Long day?"

Lying seemed like a sin in this moment. And since she was looking like his angel he knew better than to commit another sin. He wanted to touch her. Needed to feel her skin under his fingers so that he'd know, really know he wasn't alone. But he didn't want to turn her into his latest addiction. Didn't want to make her into his salvation because then they'd never be equals.

"Not really."

"Oh. Then what's up? Jeff and Alice thought you were in the men's room but I saw you come out here."

"I just needed some fresh air."

"You already said that."

"I'm saying it again."

"Well, it doesn't ring true."

"Sometimes I need to get away. You were handling things."

"Are you claustrophobic?" she asked.

"No. Not that." He rubbed the bridge of his nose. Silence fell between them. "Jeff and Alice are moving into the cigar room. They invited us to join them for cognac and cigars."

He nodded. *Of course.* Cognac was never his favorite drink, but the urge tonight was almost inescapable. He breathed deeply and clenched his hands. He would master this. The same way he'd mastered it countless times before. He was just tired tonight, his guard lowered by Corrine.

She took his hand. He didn't feel so alone anymore. She rubbed her finger along his knuckles and then dropped a kiss on his hand. "Come on. Whatever is bothering you we'll work out later."

He followed her back into the restaurant. Into the cigar room where four snifters sat. It had been a long time since he'd had anyone by his side. In fact, the last time he hadn't felt alone had been before Charles had died. He wasn't sure he trusted Corrine to stay.

He pushed the cognac aside and lit a cigar with hands that shook. Deep inside a voice whispered that one sip wouldn't hurt him. But Rand resisted, instead taking a long pull on the Cuban-style cigar.

Hell, he knew enough about fate to know she wouldn't, but in this moment he needed the lifeline she provided with her soft touch and understanding eyes. He knew he was going to have to tell her something of his past. Knew he needed to tell her before too much time had passed, but he also knew that once he did tell her, things between them would never be the same.

"Want to come in for a drink?" Corrine asked. Rand had been quiet all the way home. And though it was after midnight, the last thing she felt like was sleeping.

She was too up from dinner. Rand had put on a Steely Dan CD on the ride home. The mellow, jazzy sounds of "Babylon Sister" still played in her ears, enhancing her mood. She felt the sensuous strains of the music deep inside her.

Rand pulled into her driveway and let the car idle. He'd been in a strange mood all the way home. She wasn't sure what was going on with him.

When she'd stepped outside the restaurant earlier and found him standing there—she couldn't be sure but he seemed unsure of himself. She'd wanted to wrap him in her arms but knew he wouldn't tolerate that. He hadn't that night he'd woken from a nightmare. Frankly, she had no idea what he needed from her.

She hoped it was more than sex. But he'd been avoiding her and the doubts crept back in. Tonight she was in a weird spot. She felt at the height of her personal power—as a woman, as a businesswoman, as a lover.

Angelica had explained her relationship with Paul to Corrine one night when they'd met for margaritas. Angelica said she believed all relationships were yin and yang. Tonight she'd felt at the pinnacle of her spiritual self. Did that mean that Rand had to be at the bottom of his?

She wasn't sure.

But she sensed that sending him home alone wasn't a good idea. Besides, she wanted him to stay. She'd realized that she needed him in her life.

Even though he'd been physically avoiding her he'd called her every night to make sure she got home okay. He'd left little messages on her voice mail. It made her feel less alone in the world. And she was afraid to trust that sensation and afraid not to.

"I'll come in," Rand said. He turned off the car and walked around to open her door.

She could have gotten out of the car without him, but it was a nice gesture and one she noticed he liked to do. He put his hand on her elbow as they walked toward the house. It sounded silly even when she said it to herself, but he made her feel cherished. After a lifetime of being abandoned that was a potent feeling.

However, making her feel cherished was not all he did for her. After a mere second there was a distinctly sexual buzz in the air. Her blood started to flow more heavily through her veins and her entire body felt sensitized by his touch.

Her breasts were fuller and her breaths shorter. The scent of him surrounded her, and she realized she wanted to celebrate her successful dinner meeting in a very physical way.

She fumbled with her key and realized she was nervous tonight. The last time they'd made love he'd left. Why didn't that bother her more? She hadn't thought about it until this moment, but she realized that she expected him to leave. Everyone always did.

It wasn't just the series of foster homes she'd grown up in or the friends she'd made over the years who'd returned north when their jobs in Florida were finished. It was the entire timbre of her life. No one had ever been consistent in her life.

And she very much wanted Rand to be. But until she took the risk of letting him know she wanted him to stay, she'd never be able to get what she secretly wanted. She'd always formed emotional attachments, though she'd never wanted to acknowledge them. She'd hidden those feelings and put on her moving-on face more than once and then cried in the privacy of her own space.

This time she wanted to acknowledge her feelings for Rand. To find out if he felt the same. Then make some plans...for the future.

"The moon is nice tonight," he said. He'd taken his suit jacket off in the car and now he rolled his sleeves up.

"Yes, it is," she said, tipping her head back. The night sky shone with stars and the full moon. "It'd be a perfect night for a shuttle launch."

"I have a great view from my patio. The next time there's a night launch we'll watch it together."

She'd never been to his house. She wondered what it was like. She was still reeling from the thought that she wanted more than something temporary with him. She wanted to make a commitment to him and have him make one to her. Oh, God, what was she thinking?

"Will we still be together?" she asked. Damn, she was usually a lot better at screening her thoughts before she spoke.

He didn't say anything for a few minutes. He moved to the porch railing and leaned back against it. Despite his casual pose there was a tension in the air. "I don't know."

"Sorry. I don't know where that came from," she

said. But she did know. It came from her heart. She'd spent a lifetime ignoring her emotional impulses, but suddenly she couldn't anymore. Suddenly it seemed more important to react and feel everything that she could with Rand before he was gone.

"Don't you?" he asked. He didn't sound removed. He sounded as moved by these emotions as she was.

"I just said I didn't," she said, because she wasn't about to trust…him, she realized. She wasn't ready to lay her soul on the line on the off chance that he might be feeling something that was nearly as intense as what she was. She wouldn't let herself be that vulnerable to him. Not now. Maybe not ever.

He sighed. "I know."

She opened the front door. Her house smelled of the lilac potpourri she kept in the foyer. It welcomed her and made her feel more secure than she had only a moment before. She glanced over her shoulder. "Coming?"

"Still want me to?" he asked. She knew he needed reassurance, but she had her hands full taking care of her own battered self.

She didn't answer that. She just entered her house, set her purse and keys on the hall table and left the door open. She heard the door close but no footsteps. Damn, she was afraid to turn around to see if he was still there.

She closed her eyes and pivoted around, but didn't open them. She listened as hard as she could, tempted to open her eyes, but she didn't want to be disappointed again.

Especially not by Rand. Not this man she'd come to put all her trust in. This man whom she'd come to realize was more than a temporary lover. This man she'd come to love.

Oh, God, did she really love him?

She felt the humid warmth of his breath against her cheek and then his hands on her shoulders. Still she didn't open her eyes. Not wanting to see in his eyes pity or simple lust. In her mind she could supply the caring and affection she wanted from him. The kind of reaction that she'd give her career to elicit from him. But that she was afraid she'd never see there.

Ten

The basketball hoop behind the Corporate Spouses offices had seen more than its fair share of grudge matches. But today Rand played alone. The tension he'd always felt had grown stronger in the last month. The closer he got to Corrine the more he felt a sense of rightness. Yet at the same time he felt a sense that she was going to be his ultimate destruction.

"Telephone call, Rand," Kelly said from the doorway.

"Take a message."

"It's Corrine. This is the third time she's called."

Damn. He glanced over his shoulder at his secretary, who was wearing a skintight leather miniskirt and matching black leather bustier. Her hair was slicked back in a severe ponytail and she had long earrings dangling from her lobes. Her legs were encased in black hose and she had a pair of low boots with stiletto heels. She looked ready for an S and M club instead of the office.

"I'll be right there. Kel?"

"Yes?"

"Did Angelica talk to you about the dress code?" She rolled her eyes. "Yes."

"Then I won't say anything else."

"You better not, boss man, or I'll have to crack my whip," Kelly said before walking back inside the building.

He laughed and watched her walk away. Why couldn't he have been attracted to someone like Kelly? She was fun and sexy and she didn't cause a quaking deep inside him.

Rand walked slowly back to the building. He couldn't escape the feeling that his life was falling apart. He'd never blown off a business call before, yet he'd been willing to do it just a few minutes ago.

"Rand, I need to see you," Angelica said as he passed her office.

"I've got a call, then I'll be in."

"Thanks."

"No problem, kiddo." Angelica's pregnancy was starting to show just the tiniest bit, but that hadn't stopped her from wearing maternity clothes.

He entered his office and tossed the basketball in the corner. He was sweaty so he didn't sit in his chair but merely propped his hip against the desk and lifted the handset. His hand was shaking as he reached for the receiver.

He needed to do something about Corrine. Either give her a place of permanence in his crazy life or stop seeing her. She was making him realize some things about his life that made him uncomfortable.

"This is Rand," he said.

"Hi, Rand. Sorry to bother you at work," she said, her voice brushing over his overheated senses. He wished she were in his office so he didn't have to think and could just react. Kiss her lush mouth and caress her lean body.

"It's not a bother," he said, and meant it. She was always a welcome diversion.

"Are we going out tonight?" she asked.

"I thought so." Why was she calling? She sounded nervous, and they'd done too much together for her to be acting this way. Rand wondered if she'd picked up on his problem. Did she suspect he had drinking issues? It was way beyond the time when he should have mentioned it to her. A lot of women—smart women—didn't want to get involved with someone who had an addiction.

"Good. Just wanted to make sure. There's a new foreign film at the Enzian, want to catch it?"

"Yes. I'll pick you up."

"I'll fix dinner for us."

"You can cook?" He was surprised, because Corrine was a workaholic with little time or interest in anything that wouldn't further her career. He couldn't imagine her taking time to learn to fix food.

"Well, no, not really. But I thought I'd give it a try."

She sounded abashed and that hadn't been his intent. As always when he cared about someone, he bumbled around, unintentionally hurting them. "You don't have to. I'll pick up some sushi on my way over. We can eat in the park before going to the movie."

"Are you sure?" she asked.

"I wouldn't have said so if I wasn't."

"Sorry about that," she said with a little laugh. But it wasn't her normal one.

"What's up with you, Cori?"

Silence grew between them, and he thought she might have hung up before he heard her sigh.

"Nothing. I just want things to be right between us."

Uh-oh. This didn't sound good. "Is there some reason why they aren't?"

"Do you think they aren't?" she asked.

"I have no idea what you are asking me," he said. The only relationships he'd had with women before Corrine had been short-term, red-hot affairs. This was a totally different experience and he had no idea how to handle her in this mood.

"I guess…I've never had a relationship with someone like you."

"What's that mean?" he asked. Had she suspected he had problems that made him inadequate?

"Just that I don't want to sabotage things the way I sometimes do."

"How do you do that?" he asked. What he really wanted to know was how could *he* keep from doing that?

"I'm not sure how I do it. Just that I usually do."

"Does it have to do with your parents?" he asked.

"Maybe," she said. He heard her chair creak. "I've just never wanted anyone to stay around for a while."

"I've never wanted to stay," he admitted.

"Really?"

She needed something from him, and the tension inside him tautened to the breaking point. Could he promise her something he wasn't sure he could deliver?

"I've got to go. We can talk later."

"'Bye, Rand."

Corrine seemed to be acting strangely. Having never been in this kind of intense relationship before he wasn't sure what the hell was going on. But he hoped to God he would find out.

The movie had been really good, but then Corrine enjoyed seeing angst on the screen. Sitcoms felt foreign to her; she was a woman traveling through life on her own creating a quasifamily wherever she went.

Corrine put the coffee cups on a tray and carried it into the living room. As she did she noticed for the first time that her house—her sanctuary—was not a sitcom version of home. She'd created a place of solace for herself.

"Ready to talk?" she asked as she came into the

room. It had seemed to her earlier on the phone that they had turned a corner in their relationship. Realizing she loved Rand had made her want to put down roots.

But she'd been unable to trust herself and him enough to do that. Until now. She was ready to take the risk. Ready to jump off the cliff and hope that the water would be there. Okay, that was a cliché but it made her feel better to repeat it in her head.

Rand was standing by her wall of DVDs, scanning the titles. She wondered if he'd stumbled on her secret addiction—black-and-white romantic comedies from the forties. She stored them on the bottom shelf because one of the men she'd dated had called them corny. That might be, but she loved them.

"Sure," he said.

She set the tray on the table and then seated herself on the couch. Rand paced around the room, prowling it like a caged tiger. Okay, maybe tonight wasn't the night to take her leap.

"What's wrong?" she asked. Had she timed it wrong? Were cookies and coffee not the right thing to be serving a man when you wanted to ask him to hang around for longer than the spring?

"I'm restless. Sorry, it's a family trait," he said.

She realized she knew little of where Rand came from. Angelica had mentioned one time that his family was wealthy and Rand had mentioned a brother, but other than that she knew nothing of who he was. Where had he come from, this man she loved?

"Do you miss your family?" she asked. *Real sub-*

tle. Was it any wonder she'd never had any lasting relationships? Her skills at this type of thing were rusty at best. And of course, she'd never wanted a person to stay as much as she wanted Rand to.

"No," he said, arching one eyebrow at her. "Should I?"

She shrugged her shoulder and tugged a strand of hair behind her ear. Now would be a good time for that water to appear, she thought. "We've never talked about your family."

"What do you want to know about them?" he asked. The intensity in his green eyes unnerved her for a moment. He stopped pacing and stood near her state-of-the-art television.

"Do you like them?"

He smiled wryly. "Most of the time."

"Is it a large family?" she asked.

"I'm one of six kids. My father is one of six. My mother, one of two. Her brother is Lord Ashford, a British Peer."

She felt kind of small. She didn't know her ancestry—never would—and she'd told herself it didn't matter. Only now did she realize she'd been lying to herself. She wanted what he had. She wanted to know where she came from so that some day if she ever had children of her own they wouldn't feel so adrift in the world. They'd have an anchor linking them to past generations. An anchor that she'd never had.

"What's the matter?" he asked.

No way was she going to point out all the reasons why he shouldn't be involved with her. Corrine had learned long ago how to ignore the unpleasant parts of her life. The ones that she wanted to stay hidden. Then she focused on the parts she could control. The parts that didn't give her nightmares.

"Nothing," she said, taking a sip of her coffee and burning her tongue.

"No more questions?" he asked, sinking down next to her on the couch. Memories of the first time they'd made love assailed her. She shifted a little in her seat as lust settled heavily in her veins. Her blood seemed to run heavier and her pulse beat a little faster.

He slid his arm along the back of the couch, his fingertips caressing the back of her neck with a delicacy that made her shiver.

"Uh…I can't think when you touch me."

"Good," he said, leaning over and nibbling on her neck.

He caressed her through the thin layer of her rayon shirt and silk bra, his big hand encompassing her entire breast, rubbing with a lazy movement that made her believe he'd be happy to spend all evening on the couch petting her. She shifted, pressing her thighs together as an ache started deep inside her.

It felt as if it had been forever since he'd been joined with her. And she'd missed him. She needed to reassure herself that despite the differences in their backgrounds, Rand and she shared something very right.

"Do you really want coffee?" he asked.

She trembled with awareness and let him take her coffee mug from her hand. He hooked his free arm around her and pulled her to him. His eyes narrowed and she sensed that he was trying to distract her. But she didn't care.

When Rand touched her, the world glowed with a brightness that her dull gray life had rarely experienced. He made her feel as if there was such a thing as happily ever after and that he could be her Prince Charming.

Perhaps that was why she loved him. She didn't know. She only knew that when they were in each other's arms she forgot that she'd been abandoned too many times to believe that a man—this man—would stay with her forever. She only knew that Rand made her want to forget the lessons she'd learned early on and believe once more in dreams she'd long since stopped having.

The evening had been too intense. Actually, since that fateful February night when she'd bid on him, Rand's life had been spinning out of control. The tension inside him was wound so tight he had no reprieve from it.

Except when he was buried hilt-deep in Corrine's body. And he knew it was a crutch. A dependence he shouldn't be forming, but he was a weak man. Never before had one person affected him this deeply. Deep inside, where he hid his fears from the world, he worried that some day she'd be taken from him and his life would be nothing.

He should get in his car and head home, but he needed Corrine. Her full, luscious mouth was parted and she was sitting so trustingly in his arms. Her scent—that damned spring flower smell—assailed his senses and he knew he wasn't going anywhere on his own tonight.

He didn't question it, just lifted her in his arms and carried her down the dark hallway to her bedroom. He liked her house, felt more at home here than he did at any other place. He'd worked hard to make sure that he didn't become too connected to any place.

Here he felt comfortable for once with the illusions of who he was. He felt there was a good chance he could be the man he wanted to be when he was with her, even if he was only doing something as mundane as eating or watching television.

But tonight comfort was the last thing on his mind. He'd seen Corrine effervescent in the restaurant a few nights ago, clearly an up-and-comer in the business world. He'd seen her strong when he was weak, struggling with something she didn't understand but still offering her support. And he'd seen her when they'd discussed his family, unsure of herself.

She'd given him so much he wanted to guarantee that she would never again doubt her worth.

He set her carefully in the middle of her bed and turned on only one light—a soft one on her dresser. He opened the shades on her windows so the moonlight streamed into the room, as well.

He needed the shadows now because he wasn't sure what he felt for Corrine, but it was tearing him in two and he didn't want her to catch a glimpse of that conflict inside him. He wanted to be her hero, he realized, unable to be vanquished in her eyes.

She shifted on the bed, kicking her shoes off and stretching her arms above her head with a voluptuousness that made him harden. She'd been acting strangely since her call earlier this afternoon. Unsure of himself in this mood of hers, he knew he needed to be in control. Needed to control not only the hunger deep inside him but also the reactions of the woman who was soliciting this reaction from him.

"Where are those stockings you had on the other night?" he asked. Since he'd seen her in them and felt the lace rubbing against his skin as they'd made love, he'd had an incredible urge to use them to bind her to the bed.

"Which ones?" she asked.

"The thigh-high ones you wore that night you tied me up," he said.

"In the top right-hand drawer. Why?" she asked. She sat up on the bed and watched him.

He shrugged at her. "I'm ready for it to be my turn."

"Your turn at what?" she asked. He hid a smile as he turned and rummaged through her dresser. Corrine liked to be in control of everything and she was damned good at it. Sometimes he thought she did it too well.

"Being the master."

"The *master?*" she asked.

He arched one eyebrow at her. "What would you call it?"

"I don't know. I wish you wouldn't say it like that," she said, sounding more surly than argumentative.

"Do you object?" he asked, finding the hose in her lingerie drawer. There were several colorful scarves in the drawer as well and he removed an especially soft silk one.

"No," she said.

He sank down to the bed beside her and started to unbutton her blouse. He slid it from her body, then tossed it aside. She wore an ice-blue silk-and-lace bra. The color made her skin seem even creamier than usual. He lowered his head and tongued her nipple through the material. He teased her other nipple with his fingers, pinching it until it, too, hardened.

He leaned back to look at her. He'd never get tired of the way she looked with the red flush of desire spreading over her body. Her breaths came rapidly, her breasts strained against her bra. He removed the garment, leaving her naked from the waist up.

He wanted to touch and taste her turgid nipples again but waited for now, teasing himself with what would come. He burrowed his hands into her hair and spread the silky blond mass out on her pillows. Then, taking one of the silk hose, he gathered her wrists together and bound them. He looped the free end through the headboard, tugging to make sure the knot was secure.

"Is that comfortable?" he asked.

"No."

He checked the bond at her wrists. "Too tight?"

"No. I just feel so helpless," she said.

"Want me to untie you?" he asked. Though, seeing her bound and waiting for him had hardened him even more. He felt full and stronger. Bigger than he'd ever been before, and he wasn't sure he could take his time with her as had been his intent.

His blood was pounding in his veins, demanding he take her. Now. Instead, he took the colorful scarf in both of his hands and rubbed it back and forth across her nipples. She moaned deep in her throat and twisted again on the sheets.

She was so responsive to his every touch and there was a part of him that felt they were made to be together. Especially in the dimly lit room with the creaking bedsprings.

"Hurry up."

He chuckled and stood to remove her pants and panties at the same time. Seemed Corrine felt the same way. Knowing she needed him with the same urgency enabled him to slow his pace. He wanted to draw it out, to make this experience one she'd always remember.

She twisted on the bed, her legs moving restlessly. She looked so wanton in that moment. Her nipples standing proud and tight, begging for his touch. Her eyes glazed with sensuality.

He bent and suckled at her breast. At the same time, he slid his hands all over her body, caressing her stomach and belly button.

She called his name and he nibbled his way up her torso to her mouth. Thrusting his tongue past the barrier of her teeth, he tasted her deeply. He tilted her head back and took her mouth, not letting her reciprocate because he wanted this time to be about her. This time was for her, her pleasure first. Her pleasure above his.

She moaned deep in her throat, her hips moving restlessly against his lower body. Reaching between their bodies, he found the center of her desire and caressed her gently. She tore her mouth from his. In her eyes he saw a million words that she'd never say. Knew that the rawness he felt was mirrored in her.

"Take off your clothes," she said.

"Not yet."

"Rand, I can't wait much longer."

"Then don't," he said.

Taking her ankles in both of his hands, he pushed her legs back toward her body until she was totally exposed to his gaze.

"You're so beautiful here," he said, leaning toward her. He let his breath brush over her first. Inhaled deeply the scent of Corrine. Then lowered his head and tasted her.

She screamed. Her humid warmth welcomed him as he worshiped her with his mouth, until he felt her body gripping him, heard the sounds she made when she came echoing in the room. Then he slid up her body and kissed her deeply.

He was rock hard and needed release, but he waited until her body had calmed and started to build her again to the pinnacle. He removed his shirt and rubbed his chest against her breasts. He removed his pants and briefs and let their naked loins rub together until at last he had to plunge deep into her. Their eyes met as he thrust into her with a rhythm that drove them both to the edge.

Something deep passed between them and Rand knew he'd never be the same.

Eleven

Corrine couldn't catch her breath; she felt as if her soul had been taken from her body and it wasn't back yet. Rand untied her hands and cradled her close to him, holding her with a desperation she felt deep inside.

She knew that what they had could never last. Or could it?

Why couldn't they both stay together? Despite his wealthy family Rand seemed like the perfect man for her. He knew what it was like to be alone and she thought together they could find happiness. The kind of happiness that had always eluded her.

He made her feel everything more intensely, and though she'd never admit it out loud, she'd spent the majority of her life hiding from her feelings because she didn't want to be hurt again. But Rand had always made her feel things even when she didn't want to.

That was the reason why she'd bid on him. Why she'd taken the risk of starting an affair with him. Why she was going to take an even bigger risk... trusting him with her heart.

She'd been tired of living alone for a long time but had never found one person she wanted to share her space with until Rand. Every time he left, the house seemed too quiet. Not that he was loud or gregarious. Despite the ease with which he mingled with others, when they were alone he was happy to spend the time sitting quietly or making love.

She caught their reflection in the mirror over her dresser. He was bigger than she was and more tanned. But wrapped around her as he was, she felt he needed her as much as she needed him. Her heart was full and her mind heavy with all the thoughts that kept buzzing back and forth.

The sweat on her body was drying and she rubbed her hands up and down his spine. She loved the strength of him. Loved that he had the confidence to let her take control and didn't feel threatened by her drive or her intelligence.

The silence between them wasn't uncomfortable at all, but she needed to talk. To find a way to ask him to stay. Not just for a night but forever. And words, always her ally, deserted her.

Rand stirred against her, strafing her nipple with his fingertip. Though she'd been thoroughly satisfied, she felt the beginning twinges of desire. Before they made love again she needed to find out if he felt as deeply as she did.

"Okay, you are definitely the master," she said.

"Did you really think I wouldn't be? I'm very good at physical things," he said.

He was very good at them and she worried this was just one of the many things he had to win at. "Is sex just a sport to you?" she asked.

She didn't think so, but she needed to know now before she revealed herself to him.

Cupping her face with both of his hands, he lowered his mouth to hers and kissed her. "I'm not playing with you, Corrine."

"I'm not playing, either. In fact, I want to ask you something." She loved his green eyes, filled with satisfaction as he teased her.

"What? Want to tie me up again?" he asked. Sex had unwound him, but she remembered a few days earlier outside the restaurant when he'd been so tense. There was more to Rand then he let the world see. Maybe because she loved him she was able to see past his facade, but she suspected it was only because of their mutual feelings that she could.

As much as she'd love to spend the entire evening twisting on the sheets with him, she needed to settle some things before they went any further. She'd survived her upbringing only because she'd protected her heart. And she needed to know now if Rand was going to break her heart or help her find the kind of happiness she'd stopped believing in a long time ago.

"Rand, we need to talk."

"Maybe later. This is, um…important."

Rand said nothing, but rather lowered his head to her neck and suckled against her skin. She buried her fingers in his hair and held him to her. She loved that he seemed not to be able to get enough of her. But at the same time she recognized his actions for what they were. A diversion.

She knew that he was going to pull away again, to back away from her. She wasn't sure she could take it. She shifted away from him on the pillow.

"Rand?" He lifted his head, watching her warily. "I want to talk."

"Can't it wait until morning?" he asked, caressing her with an intent.

"No."

He sighed, then shifted around, piling pillows against the headboard and leaning against them. He crossed his arms across his chest and gave her an aggrieved look. "Okay, talk."

"Why are you so surly?" she asked.

He gestured to his erection. "One guess."

She was tempted to give up trying to talk to him and just let the moment lead them to ecstasy again. "I'll make it up to you, I promise."

"I'll hold you to it."

She cleared her throat. Now that she had his attention she was nervous. "I'm not sure how to say this."

"Just say it."

She twisted her fingers together, then shrugged her shoulders, unable to look at him when she asked him what was on her mind and in her heart. "Will you live with me?"

He jerked upright and she glanced at him. He was staring at her as if she'd suddenly grown a second head. "What? Why?"

Oh, God. Had she misjudged things? But he didn't seem disgusted; instead he seemed…afraid. But that couldn't be right. "I know we'd decided on a temporary affair, but I…I care for you and I'm tired of living alone."

He cursed savagely under his breath and stood, pacing around the room. There was a leashed violence in his movements that took her by surprise. "Maybe you should get a pet," he said.

"I don't want a pet. I've never wanted a pet. Listen, just forget this," she said, standing and grabbing his shirt to cover her nakedness. "I think you should leave."

"Ah, hell. I don't want to leave."

"Well, you don't want to stay, either." She sensed his reluctance very clearly. She knew then that he'd finally noticed whatever it was that made people leave her. He'd found that flaw, and she wanted to ask him what it was so maybe she'd stop doing it and just once someone would stay with her.

"I want to. Too damned much."

"I don't understand," she said, facing him.

"Come here."

She crossed to the bed and sank down next to him. "There are things about my life I haven't shared with you. Things that make me less than desirable."

"Rand, please. I know you're not just the fun-loving sports enthusiast that you like the world to believe you are."

"Do you?" he asked.

"Of course I do. I love you."

"Don't do that, sweetheart. I'm not the right guy for you."

"Yes, you are. I've never said those words to another person and I don't say them lightly now. But my soul recognizes you and I need you. Asking you to live with me is a big, scary step. But I think we're meant to be together."

"Corrine, you don't know what you are asking," he said.

"Yes, I do. Will you live with me?"

Deep inside Rand a part of him died. He was tempted by her in the same way that alcohol had lured him before. Not even a case of Cutty Sark could numb this feeling. His tension gripped him tighter and he fought the urge to go to her kitchen, where he knew she had brandy, and drink straight from the bottle.

In that moment, he realized he was a fraud. He'd never learned to deal with his drinking, only how to hide from it and cope with it. And Corrine had torn that safe facade away and made him face the truth of who he was.

That truth meant he could never live with Corrine. She made everything more vivid, more alive, and if she were taken from him the world would be a dull, gray place. And he'd always believed he wasn't meant to be happy. There had to be a reason why he'd been spared death. The more he thought about it, he'd come to the conclusion that his life was a penance for those he'd lost.

Happiness wasn't meant for those in purgatory. There was no way he could face his own fear that he would fail. No way that a real man would ever put a woman he loved in jeopardy. And that's exactly where she'd be. Because every day was a juggling act for him. He balanced work with an extensive amount of physical activity because it kept him busy, so he didn't have time to dwell on matters that had led him to his addiction.

He wasn't one of those people who blithely drifted through life. Each day was a struggle. A struggle not to think, a struggle not to remember and a struggle to survive. That wasn't something you invited a woman you cared about to share.

But her words touched him deep inside and he knew he'd keep them close for a long time. He thought about the long, lonely road ahead of him and knew that he would always have the memory of Corrine to warm him.

The cowardly part of him was glad she'd forced his hand now before he'd confessed his deep, dark sin. His eternal weakness that no matter how old he got he couldn't escape. No matter how much money he made on his own he couldn't buy his way out of it. No matter how often he drove home sober he couldn't forget that one lethal drunken ride.

"I can't live with you," he said at last, when he realized too much time had passed. What the hell was she thinking? He couldn't read her face; she again resembled the ice queen her co-workers knew her to be.

"Why not?"

"Some people aren't meant to have it all."

"That's bullshit."

"I wish it were."

"Are you saying that I'm not meant to be happy?"

"No. You deserve a great guy who loves you and will give you kids."

"But you're not that guy?"

"No. I'm not."

"It's me, isn't it?" she asked.

He hated that she doubted herself. Hadn't she realized anything when he'd made love to her? He'd never be able to say the words he knew she needed to hear, but he'd shown her in the only way he could how important she was to him.

"No, it's not you," he said, running his hand through his hair.

"Tell me, Rand. I can take it. I know there is something about me that makes people not want to stay. Is it the insecurity that I try hard to hide, but people see anyway?"

"No," he said. Her words cut him like tiny blades. He felt as if he was bleeding inside and knew from the pain on her face that she was bleeding, too. There was no way to make this right. No way for him to come back from the edge where he'd pushed her and himself. No safe place for him to hide anymore.

The thing was, no living person knew about his struggle. He'd hidden it for so long that he'd never really had to talk about it. Roger had known; but he'd guessed, so Rand had never had to say the words out loud. And he didn't know if he could. Even to stop Corrine from hurting, he didn't know if he could say what needed to be said.

"Is it my abandonment issues? I'm trying to get over it."

The sheen of tears glistening in her eyes made him feel like a coward. "No, baby. Stop it. It's not you."

He cradled her close, holding her with a fierceness he denied even to himself. The people who had hurt this woman deserved to pay and he could only hope they were miserable, unhappy people.

He was coming to realize what a risk she'd taken by asking him to stay. She'd said herself that no one ever had. And it humbled him that she'd taken such a risk and knew that her love for him had enabled her to do so.

Rand wished he loved her in that moment. He wished he was able to let himself feel safe enough to admit out loud that he cared for this complex, beautiful woman who'd made a place for herself in his life without him noticing.

"It's not you. God, you humble me with your bravery."

"How am I brave? I've spent my entire life hiding."

"You don't know what hiding is," he said, knowing escape wasn't going to work for him. He owed her more than a casual brush-off. He owed her the truth so she'd understand that the problem was him.

"Then tell me so I can understand."

"I need a glass of water."

"Okay."

He left her in the bedroom and walked into her bathroom. The room was neat and cheery, very much like the woman who owned it. He gulped down two glasses of water before looking at himself in the mirror. He took a deep breath and returned to Corrine.

Shutting off the lights, he left the room bathed only in moonlight. He sat on the edge of the bed with his back facing her.

"You asked earlier about my family."

"Yes."

"I need to tell you about my brother Charles for you to understand why we can never live together."

She said nothing, but he felt her shift on the bed. Felt the warmth of her body as she scooted closer to him. In his weakness he wanted to turn to her and hold her to him. To whisper his words against her sunny-colored hair so that he didn't have to hear them echoing in the silence of the room.

"Charles was my twin. We went everywhere together. Played pranks and got into trouble. We did the normal teenage things—partying, drinking, driving too fast. One night when we were sixteen, we combined all three of them and I woke up six weeks later in the hospital with a feeling deep inside me that something was gone. Charles had died instantly in the accident.''

"Oh, Rand. You were little more than a boy." She touched his back and he flinched away from her touch, knowing he still had more to tell her.

"That's no excuse. I was a Pearson and I knew what my duty was. After I was out of the hospital I returned to school. But life was different. Ah, hell, I started drinking to numb the pain and never stopped.

"I'm an alcoholic, Corrine. Since that party I've never had a drink in public because I was aware of the danger involved. But it didn't stop me from drinking," he said. He didn't tell her how he'd spent the evenings at home alone with Charles's class ring in one hand and the bottle of Cutty Sark in the other. He didn't tell her how he'd fought a battle with God and with the world. Why had Charles died?

He couldn't ask that question now. He still didn't understand why he'd survived the crash when everyone said he should have died. And the pressure of living when he knew that death should have been his had left him feeling like an empty shell. And the only thing to ever fill the void had been the booze.

"Have you been drunk since we've been together?" she asked. She still sat close to him, but she was no longer leaning toward him.

Hell, he couldn't blame her. If she'd confessed to being an animal with the scent of prey in its nostrils he would think twice about staying near her. And in effect that was all he was. He'd hidden his addiction from the world, but that didn't mean he didn't struggle with it every day, and Corrine was a very smart woman. She, more than anyone else, understood that some things never left a person.

"No. I haven't had a drink since six months after Roger died."

"Roger?" she asked. Sitting up, she crossed her legs and watched him in the dimly lit room. His shirt was draped over her, keeping her warm when he wanted to do it. This confession would be so much easier with her support. Knowing he wasn't alone. But he didn't want to make things easier on himself.

"Angelica's first husband. He was my best friend. He died in a waterskiing accident on his honeymoon." He still missed Roger. They'd spent a lot of time together even after Roger had fallen in love with Angelica. And Roger had been the only person who'd realized Rand drank. Roger never said anything but had just started involving Rand in sports and challenging him to stay sober.

"He convinced me to stop drinking in college," Rand said at last.

"You started again after he died?" Corrine asked.

He couldn't really explain it to her, but there had been that feeling of "why me" again. Why had he lived when he'd done nothing with his life? Why had he survived when he didn't have a wife? Why had he remained? "Yes."

She scooted closer to him, kneeling next to him and touching his shoulder with just the tips of her fingers. He wanted to drag her to him and cling tightly to the warmth in her, because he felt so cold inside.

"Does Angelica know?"

"No," he said, remembering that he hadn't seen her after the funeral for six months and then she'd shown up on his doorstep. Tired of living with people who thought she needed to be cosseted, she'd presented him with a proposition to combine their backgrounds and knowledge. And Rand had found a way to repay his friend for years of support and friendship by helping his widow stand on her own.

Corrine was quiet for so long that Rand was afraid to look at her—but she hadn't stopped touching him.

"I admire your strength," she said at last.

He snorted. "There is no strength in me. Every day I have to struggle with the urge to open the bottle."

She caressed his shoulder with a tender touch that made him feel exposed. More exposed than his confession had. Did she realize how much he'd come to need her?

"We all struggle with things," she said. He knew her struggle. It was in her living room lined with movies about families. It was in her cozy kitchen and her house in a family neighborhood. It was in the real Corrine that few people were ever allowed to glimpse.

"Yeah, but if you give in to your struggle you don't have the potential to harm someone," he said.

She slid down next to him on the bed, lying on her side and wrapping her arms around him. He shuddered at her touch and gave in to the urge to hold her.

"I can't see you doing that," she said.

"Sometimes I can." He slipped his hands under her shirt and traced the line of her spine.

"Rand, you've faced something that would have brought most people to their knees. The fact that you're surviving it is remarkable."

The emotion shining in her eyes humbled him but still he knew he couldn't risk it.

She'd never expected that a man as strong and in control as Rand would have something so uncontrollable in his makeup. It only fit with who he was when she looked closer at the man she'd come to know. Then on an odd level it made sense. She sensed, though he hadn't said it, that there was something he never talked about.

Her heart ached at the thought of a sixteen-year-old Rand waking up to realize his twin was dead. Her heart ached to think of how he'd struggled to fill a void deep inside. Her heart ached with the thought that her love might not be enough for him to take a chance on caring again.

She tugged him down on the bed next to her, holding him closely, needing to feel him next to her so that she'd still believe he was real. And to remind him that he was here with her in the present. He held himself stiffly and she realized now she was in danger of losing him. Before she'd only been focused on herself and her own shortcomings, ones that Rand didn't seem to see in her. It was strangely reassuring.

However, his critical eye was turned toward himself and she could do little to control what he saw.

"Is your brother's accident what you dreamed about?" she asked.

"Sort of."

Still holding himself stiff, he wouldn't look at her. "Tell me."

"I...I was driving the car, which was different because Charles had insisted on driving the night he was killed. And the car spun out of control, only this time I wasn't in the car with my brother."

"Who was with you?" she asked, though a part of her felt sure of the answer.

"You."

She shuddered. "I trust you, Rand."

"I don't."

"I still want you to stay," she said, unable to think of anything else.

Rand cupped her face in his hands. He traced the line of her eyebrows, her cheekbones and her lips with his forefinger. She held still as their eyes connected.

She felt her pulse beating a little faster. He always made her feel so feminine, so womanly, especially when she'd spent her entire life hiding that part of herself. Because that was where she'd always been the most vulnerable.

"Losing you, Corrine, would put me over the edge," he said, his voice husky and deep.

Tears burned the back of her eyes. She'd waited so long to love someone and when she did... She had no idea what to say to make him stay. But she had to try something. She started to speak, but he covered her mouth with one finger.

"Let me finish. Since Roger's death I've made sure not to form any lasting friendships. I've kept my distance from my family because there are a million little ups and downs in their lives that seem like tragedies that, if I took them to heart, might drive me to drink."

"What about Angelica?" Corrine asked, because she knew he and his partner shared a deep bond.

"She's an extension of Roger. And we struggled together to move on after Roger died. It was a difficult time for her. I had to be the strong one."

Corrine understood. Roger, because he had helped Rand, had created a bond that nothing would ever erase. And that bond extended to Roger's widow. "You're always the strong one."

"I just pretend to be." He believed what he'd said, which scared her.

"What about me?" she asked.

"You slipped past my guard while I wasn't looking."

She wasn't sure that sounded good.

He pulled her closer, tugging her head against his shoulder and leaning down, then whispered in her ear, "I care about you."

Those words lit a fire deep inside her. No matter his denials, she'd known she'd finally found a man who'd stay forever. She pulled back and took his face in both of her hands.

"You've done the same to me. All my life I've tried hard not to care and then suddenly there you were, ignoring my no-trespassing signs and making me care. Making me love you.''

''I never could resist a challenge,'' he said.

''Me, neither,'' she said, kissing him softly. ''I think we can find happiness together. Please say you'll live with me.''

He was going to say no. She saw it in his eyes. So she threw caution to the wind. She kissed him with all the pent-up desire and passion she had inside of her. ''I dare you to.''

Rand looked down at her and she clearly saw the torment in his eyes. She knew he didn't expect what they had to last, yet she accepted his simple answer. ''Okay.''

Twelve

The three weeks Rand had spent living with Corrine were at once the best of his life and the worst. The thirst for that damned unopened bottle of Cutty Sark had grown, and he woke every night in a sweat with the image of Corrine crushed in the metal hull of a car. The temptation to leave was so strong that he'd actually left her house and sat in his car twice. But both times he'd returned to her.

The pull she had over him was stronger than the need to leave. Other nights, he'd pace around her room unable to escape the portrait of horror in his head, until Corrine awoke and beckoned him back to bed. Then he'd make love to her with a desperation he only felt comfortable showing with Corrine, in the deep, dark hours of the night.

Only then could he find an escape from the feelings that dogged him. But that surcease was only a temporary one, and was soon as they were apart he'd feel again the tension from which there was no escape.

Because he couldn't go on like he was, he'd decided to try to find some closure to the past. He'd decided to fly to Chicago to visit his family. And Charles's grave. He didn't know what he'd been hoping for; maybe some sort of blessing that said it was okay to start living again—not just existing as he had been. He really wanted to make Corrine his wife, but he wasn't sure he'd ever feel comfortable enough to do it.

He'd left late Friday evening and after spending all day Saturday with the family, Rand had decided to cut his time in Chicago short. The visit had been strained. He'd found himself working harder to keep alive the illusion that he was the perfect Pearson son.

So Sunday morning, he'd kissed his mom goodbye, shaken hands with his dad and left for the airport about five hours earlier than scheduled, needing to get back to Florida and to Corrine. Being away from her had reinforced the fact that she soothed him.

O'Hare was busy as always, and the increased security was a pain, but he didn't really mind. For the first time since Charles died he felt like he belonged somewhere. And he knew that he belonged with Corrine.

It was midafternoon, but his flight didn't leave until six. He reached for his cell phone and called her. He wished he'd brought her with him to Chicago. He'd needed to be able to talk to someone, and though he and his dad had made a stab at it, in the end there were too many words to say.

"Hey, Rand," she said, most likely knowing it was him by the caller ID on her phone. "I didn't expect to hear from you until you were in Orlando. Are you?"

"No, I'm hanging out in the lounge, waiting for my flight."

"How'd it go with your family?" she asked. Corrine had thought he should mention his alcoholism to his family, but Rand had taken one look at the Lake Shore mansion and known that talking about his addiction wasn't going to happen this trip. Maybe next time. Maybe with Corrine by his side the words would come more easily.

"Same as always," he said. "What are you doing?" he asked. She sounded breathless.

"Missing you."

"Yeah?" He still wasn't used to the way she made him feel. Since asking him to move in she hadn't hesitated to tell him her feelings all the time. She was more relaxed than she'd ever been.

"Yeah," she said.

"Good."

She laughed and he let the sound roll over him. "I'm meeting Paul and Angelica for an early dinner in about an hour. Paul mentioned he wants a rematch at volleyball. Do you feel like driving over to the coast next weekend?"

"That'd be fun. He must think he can take us. We'll have to practice your moves."

"What's wrong with my moves?" she asked, laughing.

"Nothing. But practicing should be fun."

"When does your flight get in?"

"Late."

"Want me to come pick you up?"

"No. I want you in bed, waiting for me."

"I'll be here. I have some plans for you."

"Do they involve those hose of yours?"

"What do you think?" she asked, her voice husky.

"I wish I was home now."

"Me, too. I love you," she said, and disconnected the call.

She'd done that a few times. Hung up before he had the chance to say the words. Frankly, he didn't know if he'd ever be able to say them out loud to her. But in his heart he felt the words every time he thought of her. It was unnerving.

Thirty minutes later his cell phone rang and he thought this time he'd tell her how he felt. But it was Paul calling, not Corrine.

"Corrine's been in an accident."

He felt like the blood had drained from his body and his hand shook. "How bad?"

"I don't know. They airlifted her to Orlando Regional Medical Center. She's listed in critical condition. We won't know anything for a few hours."

"I'll be there as soon as I can."

Paul hung up and Rand sat down. At first he felt

overwhelmed by everything exploding inside him, but then he shoved all those emotions away and found the calm he'd always wielded as a shield in trying times.

Taking a deep breath he went to the desk and asked for an earlier flight, explaining there was a medical emergency. By some quirk of fate he got a seat on a flight leaving in twenty minutes.

Rand spent the entire flight to Orlando trying to ignore the fact that he'd been right. His gut had said he couldn't have it all. And he'd learned long ago that his gut sensed things his mind didn't.

On one level he wasn't even that surprised that Corrine's life was in danger; he'd been having dreams about it since the first night he'd spent at her place. This time he wasn't a boy facing a loss he couldn't understand, but a man with a lot at stake. He closed his eyes and whispered a fervent prayer that Corrine would be okay. Asking for help, even from God, was something he'd never been able to do, but Corrine meant more to him than anything else, even pride.

Rand arrived at the hospital just before 10:00 p.m. He was surprised to see Paul and Angelica in the waiting room. Knowing Corrine had no family, he'd been afraid she'd wake up alone. Angelica hurried to him and gave him a hug. Paul shook his hand and told him everything they knew. Corrine had a lacerated liver. They'd operated on her and now had to wait and see.

"We've been in to see her once. I don't know if

they'll let you go in or not," Paul said. Paul had an arm around Angelica. Angelica had a soft heart and he knew that she and Corrine had become good friends over the past year and half.

"I'll go check," Rand said. Rand found the nurses' station and told them he was Corrine's significant other. He was glad she'd nagged him into getting the address on his driver's license changed, otherwise he'd have had a hard time validating that claim. He realized while her life hung in jeopardy that he'd made some mistakes with Corrine.

He should have cemented his bond with her a long time ago. Regardless of what he struggled with, he was stronger with her by his side. The nurse agreed that he could visit for ten minutes, and he stalked past Angelica and Paul to enter the room.

Corrine was small and pale on the bed, her vivid eyes closed, her breath rasping in and out slowly. He bent over her, lightly touched her face, caressing her eyebrows, the line of her cheeks and lastly her lips.

She stirred but her eyes didn't open. Inside he felt a few of his emotions escaping and he was weakened by what he felt for her. He'd never told her how important she was to him. He'd never told her that he loved her. And he wanted the chance. He needed the chance, too.

He leaned over her and whispered the words that had been echoing in his head since he'd heard the news of her accident. "I love you."

Then he stood and walked out of the room. A million feelings roiled inside him and he needed to do something to get rid of the energy. He thought about putting his fist through the wall but knew in his logical mind that wasn't the solution.

When he came back out of the room only Angelica was sitting there. She watched him as he approached as if she'd never seen him before. He struggled to hide what he was feeling, running his hands through his hair.

Rand wanted to escape. To find an all-night liquor store and drink away the feelings rolling through him like a hurricane in the Atlantic. Angelica patted the seat next to her.

Rand struggled as he always did to keep his game face on. For the first time he felt it was nearly impossible to do it. Angelica held his hand tightly and didn't say anything. But he felt the love and friendship she had for him flowing over him.

He realized for the first time that although he'd thought he was keeping a wall between himself and the world, he'd created a little family in Orlando for himself.

"I never told her how I felt, kiddo," Rand said.

"Women know," Angelica replied.

"You didn't know how Paul felt."

"You're right, but I think Corrine knew. She's different with you."

"I hope so."

They sat quietly, each caught up in their own thoughts. Paul returned with coffee for everyone. When Angelica left for a few minutes to go to the ladies' room, Paul turned to him.

"You okay?"

Rand didn't know what to say. Just cocked one eyebrow at the man who'd become a friend.

"Don't let this drive you away," Paul said.

He looked at the other man and realized Paul was trying to tell him something important. "I won't."

"I almost lost my Angel because I thought life was safer if you didn't love."

Rand nodded. Angelica returned, saving him from saying anything else. Rand hadn't realized until that moment that, despite his belief to the contrary, he'd never been alone. He'd been surrounded by people who cared about him all this time.

There was a commotion in the hall and Kelly came bustling in the room. "Rand, what's the matter with you?"

"What?"

"You look unkempt. Tuck your shirt in, man. Comb your hair."

"Kel, leave the man alone, the woman he loves is in fighting for her life," Angelica said.

"Sorry. Love, eh?" Kelly asked.

Rand wasn't sure he liked everyone knowing how he felt, but he was past the point of denying it. He nodded.

"All right, boss man. I was so worried when I got that message."

She enveloped him in a hug. She continued talking a mile a minute and Rand's heart felt a little lighter. He'd never realized that families could come in so many different shapes. This one, his unexpected family, was more comfort to him than his blood relatives ever could be.

They all settled in to wait. Hours later, Kelly went out for food and drinks. Angelica and Paul left after midnight because Angelica's pregnancy was making her tired. Corrine was moved to a private room early in the morning and finally Kelly went home.

The nurse allowed Rand to sit in Corrine's room. The chair was uncomfortable, but he scooted it close to her bed and held tightly to her hand, knowing only that he needed her touch to comfort him. He hoped maybe even on an unconscious level she'd realize he was there for her. And once she woke up he planned to let her know.

Corrine woke up disoriented. The last thing she remembered was being on I-4, slowing for traffic and being rear-ended. She had a vague memory—or was it a wish?—of Rand touching her face, and she thought she remembered hearing Angelica and Paul.

She was incredibly thirsty and in a fair amount of pain. She stirred, looking for the nurse call button but stopped when she saw Rand sleeping in the chair next to the bed.

"Rand?" she asked. She was incredibly tired and was afraid she was dreaming.

He stood in a rush, knocking the chair back, and stared down at her. "Everything okay? Do you need something?"

"I'm thirsty," she said.

He checked with the nurse and then when she

okayed it poured her a glass of water. She closed her eyes again, opening them when she felt the cup against her lips. She took a swallow, then reached up to touch his dear face, so glad that he was here with her. Things must be okay if Rand was here. She closed her eyes and drifted back to sleep.

When she opened her eyes again she glanced around for Rand. The room was empty and the clock on the wall read 7:00 p.m. What day was it?

She must have dreamed that Rand had been in her room. But then the door swung open and Rand entered.

"Damn. Have you been awake long?"

"No. What day is it?"

"Monday evening. Do you remember what happened?"

"Car accident," she said.

"Yes. You had a lacerated liver. You'll be sore for a while but are on the road to recovery."

"Good."

He arched one eyebrow at her in the way she'd come to love.

"About the recovery," she said.

"Want to sit up?"

"Yes, please."

Rand adjusted the bed for her, so she was sitting. She had a moment to take in Rand's appearance. He didn't look like himself. His hair was rumpled, his shirt half untucked. She'd never seen him when he wasn't put together and she was a little worried.

Though his eyes seemed clear and aware she wondered if her accident had driven him to drink.

"What?" he asked.

She realized she'd been staring at him. "Uh... nothing. Is everything okay with you?"

"Yes." She could read nothing in his tone. She wondered if he'd stayed out of pity. She'd had her appendix out when she was twenty-three and had been alone in the hospital for three days. It was the worst experience of her life. Even if Rand was here only because of pity, she was glad.

"I didn't think anyone would be here."

"Why wouldn't I be?"

"Well...we're lovers. And I don't know—I've lived with other families before and they wouldn't have come."

He cupped her face and just looked at her for a long minute. "I thought you loved me."

"I do."

He sighed. "Listen, I'm no good with words."

She nodded.

"That doesn't mean I don't care for you."

"That's very kind of you."

"I'm not being kind," he said. Leaning over the bed, he caged her face in his hands and gave her a kiss that was sweet and gentle. Then he whispered, "I love you."

"Really?"

"Really. I can't live without you."

"Oh, Rand. I never dared to dream I'd find my own Prince Charming."

"Well, if you want to get technical, you didn't exactly find me."

"I didn't?"

"No, you bought me off the auction block."

"Lucky me," she said.

"No, lucky me. I'd been playing at living and never realized what I was missing. You've brought more to me than you'll ever know."

"You did the same for me. I love you."

"I love you, too. I'm so glad I have you. You have a family, too."

"What family?"

"Us," said Angelica from the doorway. She entered the room carrying a large bouquet of balloons.

Paul followed her with a floral arrangement, and Kelly brought up the rear with a basket of bagels.

"You have a family now, Corrine."

He smiled at her. She'd never seen such a tender expression on his face before.

"*We* have a family now."

Their family stayed for a few hours and they talked and laughed. Corrine knew that Rand was stronger because of her love and realized that his love made her stronger. She had never felt a part of the community until now, and she savored every moment. And when Angelica, Paul and Kelly left, she was also glad to have quiet time with Rand. He sat on the edge of her bed, holding her hand. They talked about the future and their dreams. Both realized that life would be full of ups and downs and only together could they weather the storm.

Epilogue

Two months later Rand couldn't believe the differences in his life and in Corrine. She'd fully recovered from her injuries and had been promoted at work two weeks later. She was now a vice president. Her job was more demanding than ever, but Rand had found that he had the power to break her single-minded focus.

He'd like to say he'd lost the urge to drink and for the most part he had. But sometimes he still felt the temptation to have just one drink, but he'd resisted. And it was easier to resist with Corrine by his side. She made him want to be better than he was.

Rand's family had visited from Chicago. He'd had a few quiet moments with his family and, with Corrine by his side, had been able to talk about the problems he had. The ones that had started long ago with Charles's death.

His father had told him that the perfect Pearson son was the man Rand had become. The words had humbled him and given him a confidence he hadn't been aware he'd been lacking. The confidence he needed to ask Corrine to be his wife.

Which he planned to do as soon as she got home from work. He'd planned every detail. Soft jazz music played in the background, the scent of fresh-cut gardenias filled the room and on the table candles flickered. He'd ordered dinner from a French restaurant in Winter Park. He had a marquis-cut diamond ring in his pocket. But that wasn't the only piece of jewelry he had for Corrine.

He had a locket with the words *Love is home* engraved on it. Inside he'd put a picture of the two of them. He paced around the room straightening the napkins and fiddling with silverware until he heard her car in the driveway.

"Rand? I'm home."

"I've got dinner ready," he said.

She entered the dining room. And he couldn't speak. Could only stare at this angel who'd come into his life when he'd least expected it.

"What?"

"You're beautiful."

She flushed. He held the chair for her. "Thanks." She noticed the jeweler's box and toyed with it.

"Open it up," he said.

"What is it?"

"A gift."

"I haven't done anything to deserve a gift."

"I'll be the judge of that," he said.

She opened the box and pulled the necklace out. She fingered it carefully and then lifted it the read the inscription. Tears clouded her eyes. She opened the locket and saw the picture of the two of them.

"Oh, Rand. Thank you."

"No, Corrine, thank you for giving me a home to call my own.

"I have something to ask you," he said.

He cleared his throat and dropped to one knee next to her. "Will you marry me?"

She smiled down at him. He felt ten feet tall when she looked at him like that. She stood and then tugged him to his feet and wrapped her arms around him. He kissed her, putting all the emotion he'd suppressed for so long into the embrace. When he lifted his head her lips were full, her face flushed and her eyes sparkling.

"Yes."

Rand let out a whoop of joy and swung her around before kissing her again. For the first time in his life he was living for himself and for the woman he loved. A woman he'd thought he'd never find.

"Good thing I'm so smart," Corrine said.

"How do you figure?"

"If I hadn't bought you we'd both still be alone."

"Bought me?"

"Really, Rand, how often do we have to cover this?"

"Just one more time so I'll know what to tell our grandkids," he said.

"Grandkids?"

"I figure we'll have at least four kids, so we should get some grandkids out of them."

"Four?"

"Will you mind?"

"No. I've always wanted a big family."

"I plan to give you one."

"I think we'll give each other one."

She was right. But then the woman he loved often was.

*   *   *   *   *

Don't miss the latest miniseries from award-winning author Marie Ferrarella:

Meet...

Sherry Campbell—ambitious newswoman who makes headlines when a handsome billionaire arrives to sweep her off her feet...and shepherd her new son into the world!
A BILLIONAIRE AND A BABY, SE#1528, available March 2003

Joanna Prescott—Nine months after her visit to the sperm bank, her old love rescues her from a burning house—then delivers her baby....
A BACHELOR AND A BABY, SD#1503, available April 2003

Chris "C.J." Jones—FBI agent, expectant mother and always on the case. When the baby comes, will her irresistible partner be by her side?
THE BABY MISSION, IM#1220, available May 2003

Lori O'Neill—A forbidden attraction blows down this pregnant Lamaze teacher's tough-woman facade and makes her consider the love of a lifetime!
BEAUTY AND THE BABY, SR#1668, available June 2003

The Mom Squad—these single mothers-to-be are ready for labor...and true love!

COMING NEXT MONTH

#1507 WHERE THERE'S SMOKE...—Barbara McCauley
Dynasties: The Barones
Emily Barone couldn't remember anything—except for the fireman who'd saved her life. Soft-spoken and innocent, she had no defenses against Shane Cummings's bone-melting charm. Before she knew it, she'd given him her body and her heart. But would she trade her Barone riches to find happily-ever-after with her real-life hero?

#1508 THE GENTRYS: CINCO—Linda Conrad
The Gentrys
The last thing rancher Cinco Gentry needed was a beautiful, headstrong retired air force captain disrupting his well-ordered life. But when a crazed killer threatened Meredith Powell, Cinco agreed to let her stay with him. And though Meredith's independent ways continually clashed with his protective streak, Cinco realized he, too, was in danger—of falling for his feisty houseguest!

#1509 CHEROKEE BABY—Sheri WhiteFeather
A whirlwind affair had left Julianne McKenzie with one giant surprise.... She was pregnant with ranch owner Bobby Elk's baby. The sexy Cherokee was not in the market for marriage but, once he learned Julianne carried his child, he quickly offered her a permanent place in his life. Yet Julianne would only settle for *all* of her Cherokee lover's heart.

#1510 SLEEPING WITH BEAUTY—Laura Wright
Living alone in the Colorado Rockies, U.S. Marshal Dan Mason didn't want company, especially of the drop-dead-gorgeous variety. But when a hiking accident left violet-eyed "Angel" on his doorstep with no memory and no identity, he took her in. Dan had closed off his heart years ago—could this mysterious beauty bring him back to life?

#1511 THE COWBOY'S BABY BARGAIN—Emilie Rose
The Baby Bank
Brooke Blake's biological clock was ticking, so she struck an irresistible bargain with tantalizing cowboy Caleb Lander. The deal? She'd give him back his family's land if he fathered her baby! But Brooke had no inkling that their arrangement would be quite so pleasurable, and she ached to keep this heartstoppingly handsome rancher in her bed and in her life.

#1512 HER CONVENIENT MILLIONAIRE—Gail Dayton
Desperate to escape an arranged marriage, Sherry Nyland needed a temporary husband—fast! Millionaire Micah Scott could never resist a damsel in distress, so when Sherry proposed a paper marriage, he agreed to help her. But it wasn't long before Micah was falling for his lovely young bride. Now he just had to convince Sherry that he intended to love, honor and cherish her...forever!